STARMINSTER

STARMINSTER

MEGAN HOPKINS

Illustrated by Devin Elle Kurtz

HarperCollins *Children's Books*

First published in the United Kingdom by
HarperCollins *Children's Books* in 2024
HarperCollins *Children's Books* is a division of HarperCollins*Publishers* Ltd
1 London Bridge Street
London SE1 9GF

www.harpercollins.co.uk

HarperCollins*Publishers*
Macken House, 39/40 Mayor Street Upper
Dublin 1, D01 C9W8, Ireland

1

ISBN 978–0–00–862689–1

Megan Hopkins and Devin Elle Kurtz assert the moral right to
be identified as the author and illustrator of the work respectively.

Typeset in Adobe Garamond Pro by
Palimpsest Book Production Ltd, Falkirk, Stirlingshire

Printed and bound in the UK using 100% renewable electricity
at CPI Group (UK) Limited

This book is produced from independently certified FSC™ paper
to ensure responsible forest management.

For more information visit: www.harpercollins.co.uk/green

Like everything
Micah and Dominic
This is for you

Map

Map

1

For days, Astrid had hoarded anything that might assist her escape from the candlelit gloom of the rhubarb shed. Silver teaspoons, a pair of blunt scissors, a burlap sack, a mug. During breakfast, she would slide them off the tray that held her porridge and under her bedcovers.

She wasn't planning to escape for long. Ideally, she'd be in and out within a couple of hours, and Mama would never know. But the Perseids meteor shower was due that very night.

Astrid had to see it.

Mama knew that the Perseids happened only once a year. She'd explained it all precisely. The falling specks of light looked like stars, but they were really just rubbish; dust and debris, shed by the Swift-Tuttle comet as it soared through the heavens.

It might be celestial rubbish, but Astrid didn't care. Even celestial rubbish was magical compared to the gloom in which she'd spent her life. Astrid wanted to see the shower of stars more than she had ever wanted anything. To belong to the thousands of star enthusiasts worldwide watching the Perseids.

And Mama had said no.

Astrid was never allowed to leave the shed. But tonight, it felt particularly cruel.

In Astrid's eleven years, she had been infatuated with koalas, then flycatcher plants, curiosity cabinets and, most recently, physics. But nothing had equalled her obsession with stars. Mama had downloaded reams of information about white dwarfs, planets, meteorites, but it wasn't enough. She needed to see the stars with her own eyes.

Five minutes after Mama said goodnight, Astrid shoved her bed to one side, revealing the soil beneath. Then she got on her hands and knees and began to dig.

She started off digging with the mug, which was quicker, but as the earth became harder, she had to start using the sharper-edged teaspoons. She emptied the soil into the burlap sack.

Progress was slow, but it didn't matter. Mama never came back after she said goodnight. Astrid had as much time as she needed.

The sound of earth shifting was loud in her ears, but not as loud as the racket that the rhubarb made. Rhubarb, unusually, crackled as it grew. It whispered and sputtered and swished, as if it were dreaming of brash daylight and rushing wind.

The rhubarb popped. The rhubarb clicked. Astrid dug.

A worm reeled out of the soil. Astrid let out an instinctive shriek. Then she lifted it up carefully, using the teaspoon, and put it on the rhubarb beds. The worm's skin was the same pallor as her own.

She dug.

Despite Mama's strict exercise regimen, she began to feel tired quickly, and her fingers blistered. She was hoping that she wouldn't need a proper tunnel. She just needed to be able to squeeze under the wall. How deep was a rhubarb shed's wall really going to be?

What was that noise?

Astrid laid her teaspoon down as quietly as she could. It sounded like footsteps, just outside the door.

What would Mama see if she came in? Astrid's dirt-smudged face. A sack full of soil. And a hole that looked unimpressive at best. But Mama would know what it meant – she would know that her daughter was trying to escape.

She'd never tried to escape before.

Astrid was a good girl. Mama said she was a good girl a dozen times a day. A good, clever girl when she completed her day of home-schooling on an ancient laptop. A good, sensible girl when she lifted her weights and ran up and down the shed. A good, mature girl, because she didn't complain often about the darkness, or the noise of the rhubarb, or the whole world that was carrying on outside the walls of the shed – the world she had no part in.

No further sound from outside. Just a tap overhead, which Mama said was the branches of an apple tree. Astrid heard it often, and she ate its fruit, raw and in pies and in tarts, but she'd never seen the tree itself.

She continued to dig. Dirt gathered in the crescents of her nails, like tiny black moons. Perhaps she'd see the moon tonight, as well. She'd seen glimpses of its faint, silver light, spilling through the doorway when Mama came and went.

Most plants need a lot of light. But rhubarb was different. Forced rhubarb, which was mostly found in and around Yorkshire, was farmed the old-fashioned way. For the beginning of its life, the rhubarb grew in fields, heavily fertilised and bathed in sun. It stayed outside until its first frost in November. Then it was transported into sheds, deprived of any natural light.

4

Astrid lived in one of those sheds. Hers had a small bathroom through a door, and a bed. But in every other way, it was a rhubarb shed.

The rhubarb preferred candlelight, so she saw everything illuminated in flickering gold. Mama's face; books, papers, artwork; her surroundings. This combination of darkness and candlelight meant that the final product wasn't ordinary rhubarb, the famously English ingredient of crumbles and fools. Not washed-out pink, barely pink. No, this was the colour of pink champagne: true pink, so sweet it sets your teeth on edge. Pink as the gasping mouths of seashells or the sky at six.

The rhubarb ticked.

It must be late by now. Maybe getting towards midnight. The hole was growing deeper.

She was almost hip deep now.

Astrid was beginning to realise that this project might take longer than she expected. Maybe weeks. As things stood, she still needed to dig under the wall, and somehow tunnel upwards without getting her clothes suspiciously filthy.

Her shoulders ached, and so did her head.

Clang.

The teaspoon had struck something hard.

Astrid thought she had hit a pebble, or maybe a tree root.

5

But as she peered into the depths of her hole, she realised that she had struck a layer of concrete beneath the walls of the shed. She prodded around with the spoon. *No.* It was everywhere.

Astrid was walled in on every side. There was no way out.

Up in the sky, not far away, the stars were falling.

Shakily, Astrid tried to pull herself out of her hole, but the dirt shifted beneath her hands. She slid back into the hole and landed with her legs twisted beneath her, the cold concrete hard against her knees.

She rubbed her face with dirty hands, and her eyes stung.

She would never see the Perseids. Never. She'd never see anything, except the candles, and the rhubarb, and the stout wooden walls. She'd never talk to anyone but her mother. She might as well not exist.

A few tears fell into the pointless hole she'd dug, vanishing. A sobbing wail broke free from her mouth. It echoed around the rhubarb shed.

* * *

Many miles south, a woman saw a dark flutter on the horizon, indistinct as smoke, and raised a pair of opera glasses to her eyes.

2

By the time Mama arrived in the morning, Astrid's bed was back in place and her face and hands were clean. She'd shoved the sack, teaspoons, scissors and mug into the hole that was now hidden under her bed.

The hole was useless now, leading to nowhere, but she didn't have the energy to fill it in. She felt its presence, even in the warmth of her bed – a void beneath her, and that concrete slab at the base.

The bolt slammed back, the door opened, and there was Mama. She held a tray with Astrid's breakfast on it, the steam curling up around Mama's head like a halo.

She put the tray down, then closed the door and locked it with the key on her belt before picking up the tray and setting

7

it on Astrid's lap. 'Good morning, darling,' she said. 'Sorry I'm a little late – I wanted fresh cream for your porridge, and Daisy was not cooperating. But I got some in the end. And look, the blackberries are ripening!'

There was a ring of blackberries around the edge of the porridge, turning the white oats purple, and brown sugar in a golden pool at the centre. Astrid smiled at the thought of the uncooperative cow as Mama poured on some cream from a little jug.

'You must be starving. You barely ate anything for dinner last night.'

She smiled over the rim of her coffee mug. Mama had a lovely face. Grey eyes that shone and crinkled at the sides like pastry when she smiled. White skin that was always suntanned or windburned, not like Astrid's fish-belly pallor. Fairish hair, always up and out of the way. No fuss for Erika Crossley, who single-handedly ran a farm in the small Yorkshire village of Lye.

'Thanks,' Astrid said. She picked up her spoon. Silver, like the one she used last night. She dug it into the porridge and took a mouthful.

It was perfect, like everything Mama made. The tang of the blackberries complemented the sweetness of the brown sugar. Creamy, hot and delicious.

But Astrid couldn't eat it. She had to fight not to gag, her stomach heaving. She would be trapped here forever, eating breakfast just like this, and never going anywhere, and never seeing the stars.

She put down the spoon.

'What's wrong?' Mama said. 'There's no rhubarb in it. I know you're fussy about it.'

'It's not that.'

Mama sighed. 'Are we going to talk about the Pleiades again, darling?'

'It's the Perseids.'

'Of course it is. Either way, I've certainly had enough of them, and nobody likes a sulky girl. Anyway, it was cloudy last night.'

Astrid looked down at her porridge. Her delicious porridge.

'When am I going to be old enough to leave the shed?' she said slowly.

'Certainly not today.' Mama held out Astrid's morning hot chocolate, topped with whipped cream and shavings of dark chocolate.

Astrid did not take the mug. 'Will you answer my question, please?'

Mama's eyebrows lifted. 'Come on, darling. We've discussed

9

this before. You'll leave the shed when you're an adult, all right? And I'll believe you're an adult when I see adult behaviour. We owe it to your development to make these useful, fruitful years. Then you won't look back and regret wasted time. So drink up your hot chocolate like my good, patient girl.' She reached out to stroke Astrid's pale, tangled hair, and said, with a touch of amusement, 'I know it's tough, being on your own so often. But other children your age are doing exactly what you're doing. School. Play. Exercise. They haven't got some glamorous life. You're not missing out on much.'

'Just the sky,' Astrid said dully.

'It's usually grey,' Mama said. 'That's England for you.'

She took Astrid's hand, running a thumb over her palm.

Astrid knew what was going to happen just before it did.

'What's happened here? Your poor little hand.' Mama turned Astrid's hand over.

Astrid pulled away.

'Blisters,' Mama said. 'Where'd you get blisters on your hands? You haven't been playing with the candles, have you? Good grief, Astrid. We've talked about the fire triangle a thousand times. You know how dangerous the candles can be, especially in an enclosed space like this.'

'It wasn't that!' Astrid blurted. Tears were welling again,

though she felt like she'd cried out every drop yesterday. 'I was – digging.'

'Digging?'

Astrid nodded, tight-lipped. A tear spilled and streaked down her face.

'Why?' Mama said.

'I wanted – I wanted to see the stars. That's all. I was never going to run away, I was going to come straight back inside – I just wanted to see the Perseids for a few minutes.'

Mama took the tray off Astrid's knee. Then she climbed into the little bed, and wrapped her arms around Astrid, and held her as she cried: tears of bitter disappointment, and of misery, and of crushing guilt. Because Mama had hurt written on her face too, though she hadn't said a word.

'I do – appreciate – everything you do. For me. I do.'

'I know you do, darling. And I understand why you dug your hole.'

'You do?'

'Of course. You wanted to see your precious stars. If only . . . but we can't, darling. It's too dangerous out there.'

'Dangerous how?'

Mama bit her lip. 'Astrid, I wish with all my heart that I could explain it to you. But can't you trust me when I say that

11

you won't understand? Can't you wait until you're a little older? I'll tell you everything then.'

Astrid sniffled. Mama gave her a linen handkerchief, and she wiped her nose.

'Here's an idea. I'll tell you what, I'll find a video of your Perseids from last night and download it so you can watch it later. Will that do?'

Mama's tone was eager, tears glimmering on her own cheeks, and Astrid ached. So instead of telling the truth – instead of saying, *No, I don't want more pixels on a screen. I want to see the Perseids myself. I want to be a part of the real world, among real people. I want to live in the farmhouse with you and milk the cow for cream and climb the apple tree and go to school with other children*, she heard her voice, quiet and a little shaky.

'Yes, that will do. That will be – lovely.'

3

Since she was nearly secondary age, Astrid had recently started the next level in her home-schooling. She would begin virtual Year 7 in September, but Mama felt that she might as well get ahead during the summer, and they could have a longer Christmas holiday together. Mama wasn't as busy on the farm in midwinter.

Astrid was practising simultaneous equations, and no matter how many times she tried one particular problem, the computer kept flashing up *Wrong! Try again – don't forget to cross-multiply!*

Mama rarely spent a full day with her. The farm was too demanding. But Augusts were especially lonely for Astrid. Mama hired combine harvesters by the day, and they were pricy, so she harvested late into the night. She always made time for

Astrid's meals, but nothing made up for the hours Astrid spent alone.

Astrid eventually solved the stubborn simultaneous equation and moved on to French. Later, she played a vocabulary game that taught her the meaning of *lachrymose* and *languish*. Which felt appropriate.

Astrid sometimes wondered if she would be totally out of step with other children when she finally left the shed. Mama laughed when she used one of her big words, or attempted a metaphor. Then again, Mama was a proud farmer who'd left school at sixteen to focus on the real world: soil, rain, crops, animals.

'I've got no time for watching TV or reading poetry,' Mama would say. 'I'm planted deep in this soil. Most people aren't rooted at all. Spend their time in the ether worrying about nonsense.'

Privately, Astrid wasn't convinced. She caught a faraway look in Mama's eyes every once in a while. A dreamy, half-present look.

She could recognise longing. It entangled every muscle in her body. It perched on her chest day and night. It never left her alone.

But Mama walked out of that door every day into daylight.

She could see the stars any evening she liked. So Astrid's opinion – although she had never said this, and never would – was that Mama didn't know a thing about *want*.

Mama dropped in briefly in the afternoon to pick up the laptop. Astrid had finished her schoolwork, and Mama had promised to download footage of the Perseids. While she waited, Astrid ran laps of the shed until she was panting, then lifted her weights and completed her yoga routine, moving through the exercises slowly and easily.

She made her bed, tucking in the sheets neatly, and cleaned her bathroom. She replaced burned-out stubs with slender new candles, toured the shed with her gardening gloves and plucked out dandelions.

Chores complete, Astrid fetched her drawing pad from the chest in the corner.

Then she drew what was in her mind: a bird with wings spread wide.

Astrid sighed. The shed felt smaller than ever. The concrete layer that she'd discovered underground shouldn't bother her like this – after all, it had been there for her entire lifetime – yet Astrid had never felt so trapped.

The squeal of the bolt, and Mama appeared in the doorway, with dinner balanced on the laptop. It slid back and forth, and some of the gravy slopped onto the laptop. 'Drat and blast it!' Mama said, wiping it clean. 'Darling, I'm sorry dinner's late. Another long day. I think they deliberately rent me the worst combine harvester of the bunch. Keeps overheating and packing up.'

'It's fine,' Astrid said.

'What are you drawing?' Mama said, peering over her shoulder. Her face froze. She took the pad and flicked through the pictures. 'Lots of birds,' she said.

'Oh. Yeah. I like birds.'

Mama touched the sketch of the bird in flight, smudging the ink a little. There was a strange, unreadable look in her eyes.

'Lovely work,' she said, putting the pad down. 'I made cottage pie.'

Astrid's appetite stirred at the scent, then returned full force. She took a large forkful, steam curling upwards, and said, 'It's delicious.'

Mama nodded at the laptop. 'Got you a couple of clips there. Taken in Montana. It slows it down, so you can see the meteorites' trails as they enter the atmosphere. I'm not a star lover like yourself, but it even gave me goosebumps.'

'Thanks.'

The rest of the meal was quiet. Astrid told Mama about the

tricky simultaneous equation, and Mama told Astrid about the workman who'd come to repair the rented harvester.

'I mean, it's a farm. You'd think he would expect a little manure. But no – the trainers got dirty, then he overbalanced and ended up flat on his face in the mud. Well, it was mostly mud.'

They both laughed, and the tension in Astrid's body relaxed for a moment.

Mama hugged her tightly before leaving.

'No more digging. All right, darling?'

'No more digging.'

'Just a peaceful night's sleep. Yes?'

'Yes, Mama.'

'I love you.'

'I love you, too.'

Mama slipped out, but a gust of wind caught the door, wrenching it from her hand. It flew wide, and Astrid saw a great blackness outside. She sat up quickly. Maybe she could catch a glimpse of the stars.

The door slammed. The bolt creaked.

Astrid lay down. Her body was warm from Mama's embrace, and she could feel the cool patch where Mama had kissed her forehead.

A few thoughts drifted through her head. Ripe blackberries on brambles. The cow that gave her milk. Stars.

She fell asleep.

*   *   *

Astrid was deep in a dream. The sky was uncertain in colour, shifting between the blue of her blankets and the grey of her mother's eyes, then shaded pink like the rhubarb. Not quite right, because Astrid had never seen the sky.

A sound, and the dream ruptured.

She lay, half dreaming, wondering if she'd imagined the squawk of the bolt.

Then a rustle, nearby.

Astrid opened her eyes. For the first time in her life, the person looking down at her was not her mother.

The unfamiliar face was jarring – she had only ever seen other faces on a screen. The woman wore bold make-up against her dark-brown skin, lips bright in the dim light. A pair of brass opera glasses dangled from her belt, and she was stowing a long silver tool in her pocket.

The woman's scent was sweet, but not in the same way as Mama, who was flavoured with vanilla and rosemary and cinnamon and cloves, all the perfumes of the kitchen, with an undertone of rain and damp soil. This woman smelled intoxicating, like maraschino cherries.

But the truly astonishing thing was the wings folded over her shoulders.

Astrid blinked at the turquoise feathers that blended into the woman's silk dress. Were they real, or some sort of costume?

She shrank back.

'Who – who are you?' she said. Her voice was scarcely louder than the rhubarb.

'My name is Mrs Wairi,' the visitor said. 'And yours?'

'Astrid,' she whispered. 'What are you doing here?'

'Is this where you live, Astrid?'

'Yes.'

'Permanently?'

Astrid nodded. 'How did you know I was in here?'

Again, Mrs Wairi ignored her question. 'What happened last night?'

How did she know?

'I – I tried to dig.'

'To dig,' Mrs Wairi repeated.

'To dig my way out.'

'I see.'

Astrid couldn't tear her eyes from the woman's face. It was

usually easy to guess what Mama was thinking or feeling, but this woman was impossible to read.

'Why didn't you succeed?'

'Succeed?'

'When you were digging.'

'Oh. There's concrete. Down there. You can't dig your way out.'

Mrs Wairi paused. 'Do you know that it is unusual to live in a shed?'

'Yes. It's – it's dangerous outside.'

'I see,' Mrs Wairi repeated. 'But you would like to leave.'

Astrid looked down at her hands, tugging a loose thread on the duvet cover. 'I just want to see the stars,' she said. 'Can I ask about – about your wings?'

'If you wish.'

'Do they work? Can you – fly?'

'Yes.' Mrs Wairi smiled.

Astrid pondered. On the whole, this was difficult to believe. But on the other hand, her wings looked so real, the feathers glistening in the candlelight. Astrid wanted to run her hands along them. Real wings, just like the ones on the computer screen. Like on the birds she'd drawn, but better, brighter.

'No one can fly,' she said.

'You're wrong about that, Astrid. But it's certainly a common misconception.'

The light swam before Astrid's eyes, and the hair rose on the back of her neck.

'Are you an angel?'

'Not in the slightest,' Mrs Wairi said. 'I am a Librae. So are you – or you will be one day.'

Astrid swallowed. For a heartbeat, she pictured herself with wings – imagined her feet lifting from the ground . . . imagined diving into the sky.

The hope within her felt hard and bright, a pebble of star debris.

'I'll be able to fly?' Astrid whispered. 'You promise?'

'I promise. But first, you'll need to leave the shed. I'm here to take you away.'

'Take me where?'

'To London Overhead. It's a city for people like us. For Librae. Will you come with me?'

'I don't – I don't know.'

Mrs Wairi reached out and touched a pink stalk of rhubarb, running its fragile yellow leaves through her fingers. 'Is this rhubarb?'

'Yes.'

'I see.' She let go of the plant, and looked at Astrid, her gaze forceful. 'Astrid, I know you're afraid. But a lifetime is too long to stay hidden in a shed. So will you come?'

When blaming a celestial body for madness, the moon is the usual culprit. But Astrid's mind was full of the night sky, and the sparkle of stars. The Perseids meteor shower hadn't quite ended. There was still a chance she could see it for herself.

'I'll come,' Astrid whispered.

Perhaps on another night, Astrid would have resisted when Mrs Wairi helped her to her feet and escorted her across the shed. But she had wept in a dead-end hole in the ground last night. She was hungry to watch the Perseids slashing across the sky.

Astrid followed Mrs Wairi through the doorway.

Behind her, the concussive slam of the door.

4

Astrid stood on shaky legs outside the threshold. She shielded her eyes with her hands. It was already too much, too much.

The air was moving.

Astrid had never felt wind like this, the air yanking on her with intent. Her fair hair spread out; her heart jolted. She gulped a lungful of swelling air.

The stars. She was going to see the stars, at last.

She wasn't sure what to expect. In nursery rhymes, they twinkle-twinkled. Pictures rendered them static, though numerous; film turned them into a depthless plane like a sparkly Christmas card. She had seen pictures of galaxies like an opal necklace, gleaming a hundred colours; white flame wreathing the surface of a ball; the Milky Way like a pathway to heaven.

Astrid put out one hand to brace herself against the frame of the door, and looked up.

She couldn't see them. Her sight was blurred, and the sky just looked dark. She couldn't see a single individual star.

She'd left the rhubarb shed. The sky, a void. And her eyes wouldn't work – she couldn't even see the stars. Couldn't even see the apple tree, or Mama's fields.

The wind rose, panting in great gusts, plucking at her pyjamas, tugging at the hair on the back of her neck, an invasion that she could hardly bear. Instead of gentle candlelight, the lurid white gleam of the moon.

'Are you all right, Astrid?' Mrs Wairi said from a few steps away. Her voice was swept away by the wind, and it came to Astrid's ears only distantly.

It would be morning soon. Her mother would come into the shed with breakfast, and sing out, 'Darling!', and the bowl would tumble to the floor and explode into fragments, and Mama would tear through the blankets on the bed, and she would howl Astrid's name, over and over. Perhaps months would pass, and Erika Crossley would sit at the kitchen table every night with useless tears slipping down her face—

Terror sprang up within Astrid, mounting by the moment, her heartbeat loud and erratic in her ears.

'I can't do this,' she said.

She tried to hurry back into the shed, tripped on the unfamiliar gravel and fell on her hands and knees. Mrs Wairi helped her to her feet, and she tried to pull away. 'I want to go back,' she said, the words tumbling out in a torrent. 'I don't like it out here – it's too strange – I can't leave Mama!'

Mrs Wairi's grip was strong as steel.

A scream rose up like vomit and burst forth. She thrashed. 'Let me go!'

Astrid almost broke free, reaching back for candlelight and the crackle of rhubarb. Then a hole opened below her, no concrete blocking it, and Astrid fell through the hole into blackness.

* * *

Astrid woke to a rhythmic purr, vibrations in her bones.

She was in the front seat of a car. No tapping, no clicking. No rhubarb. No walls around her. And the scent was different – a synthetic smell, like bleach or weedkiller.

Mrs Wairi was driving, her eyes fixed on the road. Astrid's limbs were heavy. Everything seemed muted, as though seen through a screen. Shapes and colours rushed past the window.

'What . . . ?'

'You fainted,' Mrs Wairi said.

The car's motion made her squirm, nausea stirring in her stomach. It was dark, but there were tiny lights and dials in front of the steering wheel. Outside, beams of light moved through the blackness. A digital clock read 5:23. Hours had passed. Mrs Wairi must have been driving through the night, Astrid asleep beside her.

'I want to go home,' Astrid said.

'That's understandable. But what we want is not always what's best for us.'

There were tears trickling down Astrid's cheeks. Her arms were too weak to wipe them away.

'My mama . . . I want her,' Astrid whispered.

'Would you like to tell me about her?'

Astrid found herself nodding.

'What is her name?'

'Erika Crossley.'

'She looks after you, brings you food?'

'Not just food!' Astrid said defensively. 'She brings me everything I need.'

'And what do you need?'

'Well, I do school. On a computer. And I read books and play games and draw pictures. Sometimes we watch documentaries and twenty-four-hour camera feeds of all the places we wish we could go. I know it's weird. To live in a shed. But Mama loves me. I told you, it's . . . dangerous, outside. She protects me.'

Mrs Wairi didn't glance at Astrid when she said quietly, 'Not much of a life for a child.'

'It is,' Astrid insisted. 'It's like other lives. Just a bit . . . smaller.'

'That's one way to look at it,' Mrs Wairi said, her voice bland. 'But you mentioned that you tried to dig your way out recently.'

'I mean, I did, but I only wanted to go out for an hour,' Astrid muttered.

'You found an underground layer of concrete. You realise what that means, don't you?'

Astrid tilted her head. It didn't mean anything. Did it? 'No.'

'It means that the shed was built to hold you.'

Astrid stared at her. 'No,' she said. 'That's not right.'

'There's no reason to line a shed with concrete. And I can assure you that the other outbuildings on the farm are not nearly as secure as yours.'

'You mean – you mean Mama – she made the shed? For me?'

Mrs Wairi nodded.

Astrid's hands clenched. 'She never told me that.'

Her mind was racing, trying to reject this new idea – that Mama had built a place to keep her. Astrid had always assumed that the rhubarb came first, and that Mama had thought of it as a safe place to hide her daughter; that her little bathroom, off the main shed, was a later addition. It clearly wasn't. Mrs Wairi's words made sense.

Why couldn't Mama have built her a home, then? Why couldn't Astrid have had a bedroom like the ones in films, with a carpet and a window and a cosy little bed? Why'd she have to live like some sort of rural Cinderella?

Mrs Wairi was speaking again.

'The farm is your mother's property, I presume?'

'I don't know. She talks about a mortgage.'

'Ah.' Mrs Wairi pressed a lever. The car clicked, a light flashing on and off. Astrid twitched. It sounded like rhubarb. 'She does own it, then. She bought it with a loan. Does she farm it herself?'

Mrs Wairi turned the steering wheel, and Astrid felt the car obey, pulling her to one side. The clicking stopped.

'Yes,' Astrid said. 'And what are – what are you? You said you're a – Librae?' She stumbled over the unfamiliar word. 'You don't mean a Libra? Like the zodiac sign? That's – that's my sign, I think.'

'I certainly do not mean a Libra,' Mrs Wairi said. 'A common misconception with those new to our kind, and I'd advise you to put that out of your mind right now, Astrid. I am a *Librae*. But that's not quite the same as being a farmer. I'm a Librae in the same way that I'm Black. Born that way. When is your birthday?'

'The twenty-third of October.'

'Just in time, then. Only a minuscule percentage of the people born between the twenty-third of September and the twenty-third of October become Librae. Their chances of fledging – that is, growing wings – are far greater if their parents are Librae too.'

But Mama wasn't a Librae, and who knew about Astrid's anonymous father?

'How do you know that I am a Librae, then?'

'I have my ways,' Mrs Wairi said.

Astrid noticed that Mrs Wairi's wings had vanished.

'Where did your wings go?'

'They retract inside my shoulders when I need them to.'

'Are mine inside my shoulders too?'

'Children don't get wings until they reach a certain age. Around twelve, as a rule. You're how old?'

'Eleven. So in a year or two . . . I'll have wings?'

'Yes,' Mrs Wairi said, looking over at her. 'Won't that be wonderful?'

Astrid reached over and touched her shoulder blades beneath her T-shirt. Would wings force their way out from the skin one day, and carry her into the sky?

Gradually, the sky was brightening. The daylight was horribly pale. The shadows, back in the rhubarb shed, were soft-edged, always doubled or tripled. Here, they were sharp as glass.

Astrid peered out of the windscreen. For the first time, she could focus a little. A furry green triangle coalesced into a tree. What an astonishing thing it was! Leaves dancing in the faint sunlight.

Sunlight. Mama would be awake by now. She would have started to make breakfast. Poached eggs, maybe, with hot buttered toast.

Soon she would go to the shed. She would find her daughter gone.

'I'd still rather go home,' she said.

Mrs Wairi shook her head. 'You're the first child I've met who's said no to flying.'

'Have you met lots of children, then?' Astrid asked, unable to hide her curiosity.

Mrs Wairi smiled, her teeth white and perfect. 'Yes, indeed.

In fact, in the same way that your mother's job is to farm, my job is finding Librae like yourself. Unfledged Librae children.'

'Unfledged, meaning – no wings yet.'

'Precisely.'

The car slowed to a crawl, ticking and turning around bends and corners. Not much green outside now – grey boxes, instead, some huge. If she strained her eyes, squinting hard, Astrid could see skyscrapers alongside wedding-cake townhouses and Gothic churches, the architecture of centuries jostling up against one another. Her head began to ache, and she sank back in the seat.

'We're not far from London Overhead now.'

'Where's that?' Astrid asked.

Mrs Wairi smiled, and pointed upwards. Astrid leaned forward and craned her neck.

'You won't be able to see it just yet,' Mrs Wairi said. 'It's hidden, of course.'

'My eyes aren't working too well. It's all so bright.'

The car slowed, and Mrs Wairi turned to look at Astrid again, her searching gaze making Astrid long to hide her face.

'Mm,' she said eventually. 'Probably to do with the shed. You've never had to focus on things more than a few metres away. Could be the light, as well.'

'Do you think I need glasses?' Astrid asked.

'Not necessarily. It's probably just about building up the strength of your eye muscles. Practice makes perfect.'

Astrid frowned. She'd always been able to see perfectly in the rhubarb shed. It had never occurred to her that living there would damage her eyes. She wondered whether Mama had known it would. And what other damage might be lurking, unseen, within her.

Something else was tugging at her attention, though she wasn't ready to face it yet. The unnamed danger that Mama had kept her hidden away from. What had Mama been so afraid of?

Astrid had only been out in the world for a matter of hours, but it didn't *seem* like a dangerous place.

Or – was the danger *this*? Mrs Wairi – the Librae?

Had Mama known about Librae? About wings?

Surely not. She would have told Astrid. Mama was honest with Astrid, always. Or was this whole secret world the mystery that Mama had always promised to reveal when Astrid was older?

'Where *exactly* is London Overhead?' she asked.

'The city is mostly above the Square Mile. Londinium, as it was in Roman times.'

A city above a city. The scientist in Astrid wanted to protest that it was impossible, nonsensical. 'How are we going to get up there when I can't fly?'

'You'll see.'

The car dawdled through traffic lights until, at last, Mrs Wairi drove into the mouth of an underground car-park. The daylight faded away, replaced with the shivery glare of fluorescent tubes. They parked up and got out of the car – Mrs Wairi had to help Astrid undo her seatbelt – and took a staircase up to the street.

It was so crowded that Astrid froze, her stomach roiling with astonishment – or was it terror? Everything she saw was new. People marched up and down the pavements, their steps as assured as a dancer's. Astrid wondered how it would feel to walk among others without hesitation. To dissolve into a crowd like a molecule, join conversation, and saturate herself in the company of others. To belong.

'Here, take my hand,' Mrs Wairi said.

And before Astrid knew it, she was part of the crowd, walking in step with dozens. She glanced up every so often, into that labyrinth of other people, their shoes tapping on the concrete. Quick scenes flashed before her vision: a square lined with restaurants, a man playing the saxophone with a box of coins at his feet, the eye-catching reflection of sky from a wide river.

A thrill of excitement, her heartbeat accelerating. This was what she'd been missing. A hundred faces, notes of music breathing forth into streets, a burst of laughter from passers-by. Her childhood could have been filled with moments like this. Instead, those dark, empty years yawned behind her, like a chasm.

At last, they reached a narrow street. Mrs Wairi stopped at a sign reading 'Shangri-La'.

'Don't strain your eyes too much, Astrid,' Mrs Wairi said, 'but have a look up.'

Astrid tipped her head upwards. The glass tower kept on going, up and up until her neck hurt, and the skyscraper was swallowed by cloud.

'W-where are we?' Astrid said.

'The Shard,' said Mrs Wairi. 'The tallest building in London. Come along.'

Astrid obeyed, following Mrs Wairi into a passageway, where she immediately relaxed. A ceiling over her head, like a warm blanket. No infinite void above her. 'Unfledged people usually enter London Overhead from one of the taller buildings,' Mrs Wairi told her as they walked up a staircase. There were signs everywhere, reading 'The View From the Shard', with pictures of London at its most stereotypical, telephone boxes and black cabs galore.

They passed through a security system, all metallic gleams and bleeps, and were stopped by a man in uniform. 'I'm afraid the viewing platform is closed at present,' he said.

Before Mrs Wairi had time to reply, a woman hurried over, saying, 'Welcome, Mrs Wairi. We've had the platform cleared in preparation for your visit. Please follow me.'

They stepped into the lift. The interior was mercifully dim, and they watched a display of numbers as the floors blinked by faster than seconds. It made Astrid flinch, the speed of the lift swooping up the building.

The lift stopped.

The woman moved out of the way, bending her knees in something that was almost a curtsey. Astrid trailed after Mrs Wairi into a second lift, from which they disembarked onto a platform. The platform was surrounded by glass but open to the elements, and Astrid's arms tingled in the chilly air.

'I don't think you should try to look at the view,' Mrs Wairi said. 'It might make you dizzy.'

But Astrid couldn't resist. She narrowed her eyes, and it swam into focus. A miniature city, spread at their feet.

She pressed her palms against the glass and squinted out –

first west, then north, leaving ghostly handprints on every pane. Astrid recognised the icons of London, familiar from her computer screen. The Eye, as if London were a carnival in full swing. The towering timepiece of Big Ben. Bridges twined the sluggish Thames; Tower Bridge swarmed with scarlet double-decker buses, small as ladybirds.

Astrid turned back to Mrs Wairi.

'I don't understand how people live up here. There's no city above London.'

'You can't see London Overhead yet,' Mrs Wairi said. 'We have to wait for your authorisation first. Good morning, Councillor Paulson. Thank you for bringing the Ceramicists' essence.'

Astrid looked around. No one was there but her.

'I do beg your pardon, Astrid,' Mrs Wairi said. 'A Librae gentleman has just landed. I'm afraid he is currently invisible to you.'

Astrid blinked up at her suspiciously. 'Right,' she said.

Mrs Wairi stretched out her hand, and a tiny pot appeared. It was filled with what looked like mud.

'Please apply the substance to your eyes,' Mrs Wairi said.

'What's it for?'

'It will allow you to see the city, and the Librae living there.'

Astrid felt a breath against her neck. Again, she turned her head, but no one was there.

'In my eyes?'

Mrs Wairi nodded.

Astrid hesitated, then daubed the mud into her eyes. It stung. She scrubbed at her eyes furiously with her sleeve. 'How does it work?' she asked.

'The Ceramicists . . .' Mrs Wairi paused. 'I don't want to overcomplicate matters. The mud will allow you to see the city. It should take effect any moment now. If you would step back over to the glass?'

Astrid placed her hands neatly over the outlines her fingers had left minutes before. The sun lay dormant somewhere overhead, a wan phantom. She looked out at the carpet of London, screwing up her face to focus as hard as she could, and waited.

The picture didn't leap into existence, or fade in like music. It arrived in glimmers, like lights turning on in windows as night falls. And Astrid saw a city most of the world would never see; a city for the winged: London Overhead.

5

The net appeared first. Diamond patterned, gossamer, it seemed to weave itself before Astrid's eyes, dividing her from the view below.

She blinked.

Gigantic flower-shaped buildings leapt into existence, towering over everything else, almost the height of the Shard. Nearby, a rose, a dahlia and a stargazer lily pointed to the sky.

But the flowers were only the beginning. Bridges – thousands of them, surely; bridges of gleaming steel cable, rope bridges, stone bridges. Bridges connecting the flowers; bridges like pathways between platforms. And staircases too – straight, zigzag and spiral.

'It's magnificent,' she breathed.

The sun came out. The Thames was molten; water like liquid gold. At Astrid's feet, a toytown: nothing compared to the city that sprawled in the sky like the world's most elaborate spiderweb. She felt a tremor of delight and awe.

The Londons combined to create a bewildering chaos, a city in three dimensions and on hundreds of levels – some only steps below the tip of the Shard, some almost brushing the city below. Astrid could hardly make sense of it, nor of the staggering elation that filled her.

Above, a handful of gliding birds. Astrid gazed at them. The first birds she had ever seen. How peaceful they looked in the sky, as if flying were nothing. Her sketched birds had never captured that. Their freedom. Their ownership of the sky.

'Right,' said someone behind her. 'Shall we go down?'

Astrid started, spinning around.

'I do apologise,' the man said. 'We haven't been formally introduced, of course. My name is Councillor Paulson.'

Astrid's mind told her *angel*, though she knew that angels didn't wear tailored suits, or paisley ties, or gleaming leather brogues. He had pearl-grey pigeon wings and carried a ladder under one arm.

He shook her hand.

'Councillor Paulson is in charge of immigration and infrastructure in London Overhead,' Mrs Wairi said.

'Why couldn't I see him before?' Astrid asked.

'It's to do with the Ceramicist enchantment that keeps the city hidden. Once you put the Ceramicist mud in your eyes, the city appears to you, and within it, you are also invisible to people in London Underfoot. The net marks the boundaries, so Librae who fly beyond the boundaries have to be very cautious to avoid detection. London Overhead is a haven. Outside it, we have to be very careful about when we deploy our wings. But enough of that. Councillor, would you set up the ladder?'

'Certainly,' Councillor Paulson said. He unfolded the ladder and set it up against the wall.

Mrs Wairi took Astrid's hand and helped her onto the bottom rung. She balanced with difficulty. This wasn't a skill that had been required in the rhubarb shed. Her stomach swooped and twisted.

When Astrid reached the top of the ladder, the wind increased in strength. She climbed carefully onto a stairway of glass that mimicked the architecture of the Shard. The steps were translucent, and Astrid's insides pirouetted in protest. She reached for the flimsy glass handrail. Mrs Wairi was soon next to her, dress billowing. Without speaking, she took Astrid's hand and clasped it tightly.

'Keep your eyes on the next step, Astrid,' Mrs Wairi said.

Below, the net shimmered in the sunlight. It didn't look like it could hold someone like her, let alone someone the size of Councillor Paulson.

'Surely it's dangerous up here,' Astrid said. 'For people who can't fly, I mean.'

'I suppose it is,' Mrs Wairi said, with an air of faint surprise. 'You'd be surprised how strong the net is, though.'

It was like Mrs Wairi had read her mind. Suddenly she was full of questions. 'Where will I live?'

'Most of the London Overhead citizens live in nesthomes. Tents, really.' She stopped walking and pointed at the rose nearby. 'See those black things dangling from the Seventh Flower? They're nesthomes.'

'Do nesthomes have toilets and kitchens and all that?'

'Not always,' Mrs Wairi said. 'That sort of thing is managed communally.'

Astrid wasn't sure what that meant. 'Where do *you* live?'

Mrs Wairi paused. 'I don't live in London Overhead, actually,' she said at last, her voice almost drowned out by the blast of the wind. 'But I do visit, from time to time.'

41

'Who will look after me, then?'

'There's a children's boarding house on the Fourth Flower for those who don't come with their parents. There are lots of other externals there.'

'Externals?'

'Young people who don't have Librae parents.'

Astrid hesitated. 'Can't my mother come and live somewhere in London Overhead with me?'

'Non-Librae parents don't live with their children. It can be distracting. We like our new students to focus on learning to fly, on becoming citizens of London Overhead. London Overhead is yours now. You belong here. How can that possibly compare to the dark shed where you were raised?'

When Astrid didn't respond, the adults swept away onto a filigree iron bridge arcing into the sky. Tentatively, Astrid followed.

The wind sighed, and Astrid shivered. She couldn't get used to the intrusive breath of air on her neck. Atop a building shaped like a walkie-talkie, a star-patterned blue-and-gold tent was rippling in the breeze, transforming it from sophistication to circus. Again, her mouth fell open in wonder.

At the next crossroads, Mrs Wairi paused to gather up her long skirt and stepped onto the first plank of a rope bridge, her sharp stiletto heels tapping on the wood. Councillor Paulson sent the bridge swaying with his bouncing step, and Astrid followed, clutching the rope.

Two Librae swooped past, their wings glorious.

Another turn, onto a stone bridge that looked a century old. It was slippery with moss, and the railing was missing at intervals. At the corner, there stood a map of London Overhead, the bridges crisscrossing, labelled with tiny script. The map, like the landscape it depicted, was dominated by the huge flowers, labelled with numbers one to twelve. Astrid's eyes caught random place names: 'The Department of Belfries', 'The Bridge of Whys', 'Seven Stairway Square', 'Minaret Parliament'. A tiny light shone in the top left corner of the map – Astrid leaned closer to read, 'You are here'. The bridge where she stood was called 'Crumbleton Way', a name which made her nervously scurry after Councillor Paulson when he called her to hurry up.

The next staircase was so steep that Astrid had to climb down backwards, Mrs Wairi close behind her. The London that had been a carpet under her feet grew closer as they lost altitude, some of the skyscrapers protruding into London Overhead. The city grew busier.

Most Librae flew, gently skimming a dozen or so feet above

the main bridge thoroughfare. Commuters, mostly, if their briefcases and office wear were any indication.

'What are all these people doing?' Astrid asked, her pace slowing. Her muscles and lungs burned, and perspiration was cold on her face.

'Going to work. Half of the Librae in London Overhead have normal jobs. But the other half work with the Overlords. Managing education, health, the treasury. Avoiding any hint of modernity or, heaven forbid, technology in London Overhead.'

Astrid caught the brittle note of sarcasm in Mrs Wairi's voice.

'Overlords?'

'The government, more or less. They're in charge of London Overhead and Librae England generally.'

'Doing what?'

'We're custodians of the sky, Astrid.'

Astrid liked that phrase. She mulled it over, then said, 'What does that mean?'

'Mostly, over the last century or so, we've been seeking to reduce pollution.'

She pointed over to a dark blot on the horizon. 'A sky forest over Canary Wharf. We've planted hundreds of them around the world, hidden from the sight of the people below and maintained by the Librae, absorbing carbon dioxide and giving out oxygen. Returning our skies to the way they used to be. I will admit that some technological advancements – in London Underfoot, at least – have been far from positive.'

Astrid stopped again, closing her eyes and focusing on the wind. She'd hated it at first, the motion, the intimacy of it. But it felt cool against her hot skin. Cleansing, somehow, as though it were blowing away the cobwebs of a lifetime confined.

'It's beautiful up here,' she said.

'This is one of many Librae settlements, Astrid. They're the last places in the world where we can fly freely, unseen.'

Fly freely. Another phrase that filled Astrid's heart with delight.

'Where are we going now?' she asked.

'To visit the Headmaster,' Councillor Paulson said.

'There's a school up here?'

'Yes. Starminster is a school of flight. You probably know it as St Paul's Cathedral. It's the only building that Underfooters and Overheaders both use. They have it in the day, but at night, it belongs to us – it's part of both worlds.'

'You'll attend it yourself,' Councillor Paulson added.

'Why do we have to learn to fly in there?' Astrid asked.

'It's too dangerous for Librae who've just fledged to fly in the open air. They need time to gain in skill and confidence before facing things like wind currents.'

The dome of St Paul's Cathedral grew larger as they approached, casting a shadow over them.

'Starminster will be opening to the London Underfoot public shortly, so most of the students are heading home now,' Mrs Wairi said.

Astrid saw a group of children – *children*, the first she'd seen – standing on a balcony on the top of the dome. A teacher was bellowing instructions. As she watched, their wings broke through their clothing and unfurled. Their wings were all different – some brown and speckled, like the wings of sparrows, others tropically bright; some glossy, others dull; some wingspans immense, some shorter than the bearer's outstretched arms.

Then they lifted off, zigzagging, swooping, the teacher in the lead.

The dome of Starminster was lone and splendid against the morning blue.

6

They took an ancient set of stone stairs, almost as ornate as the cathedral, and went down onto the gallery that surrounded the dome like a collar.

'The Headmaster will meet us in the clock tower,' Mrs Wairi said.

They didn't go inside, instead taking a set of stairs to a walkway that led past the edge of the sloping roof. There were two towers, side by side, populated by statues that stared blindly out at the London skyline. The clock's golden hands were more like arms, pointing the time. It was now twenty minutes past six.

Mrs Wairi paused to knock on the clock face itself.

'Enter!' came the reply, and slowly, the great clock swung open.

Inside, machinery was ticking, and great wheels were turning.

Amid the wheels and the cogs and the ticking, a man sat at an antique desk writing on a piece of paper.

The ticking made Astrid flinch. It was so like being in the rhubarb shed, that unending rhythm.

The man was old – or was he? He had hair peppered with white, and the bags under his eyes bulged, but his stance, when he got to his feet, was youthful.

'A new student, Mrs Wairi?' he said. 'Excellent. Good morning to you. Your name?'

The ticking was distracting. 'Astrid,' Astrid said, then realised she'd spoken very quietly. 'Astrid,' she repeated.

There was a glass display case in a corner, and inside it, stuffed birds gazed balefully out at them.

Mrs Wairi followed Astrid's gaze.

'Mr Finifugal is a biologist, Astrid. His specialism is avian anatomy. He's studying Librae physiology.'

'That's . . . that's interesting.'

'It certainly is,' the Headmaster said briskly. 'Now, you'll be joining us tomorrow night, I trust. Your timetable is here.' He handed her a sheet of paper. 'Promptly to lessons, and do try your best, won't you?'

Astrid nodded, then, catching Councillor Paulson's critical eye, said, 'Yes, sir.'

'This is the opportunity of a lifetime,' Mr Finifugal said. 'Millions of children would do anything to be in your position. So don't waste it, eh?'

'No, sir.'

'Off you go, then.'

Astrid moved out of the way of Councillor Paulson as they headed back towards the clockface door, and accidentally brushed against the glass display case. It wobbled, and a bird fell off its perch, its glassy eyes staring directly into Astrid's. Not just glassy, surely – they had to be made of actual glass, or they wouldn't shine like that, not when the bird was dead.

Astrid's head was hot, her heart pounding in her ears. She swayed.

'Something odd about her eyes,' Mr Finifugal muttered to Mrs Wairi. 'Is she quite well?'

'Headmaster, please,' Mrs Wairi said, her voice tight, but Councillor Paulson tapped her on the shoulder.

'Mrs Wairi, he's right. Look at her.'

Astrid wasn't sure why everyone was staring at her, but she knew that the pain in her head had tripled, that the birds in the case were dead, and that Mama had found the shed empty now. That Mama was crying.

'Astrid, your pupils are uneven,' Mrs Wairi said, her face

close. Astrid could see tarry flakes below her eyes, shed mascara. 'Do you need to sit down?'

'Not here,' Astrid said unsteadily. Her face was wet, though she wasn't sure if it was tears or perspiration.

'Come on,' Mrs Wairi said, putting her arm around her.

When they were outside again, Councillor Paulson shook hands briskly with Mrs Wairi and flew away. Astrid stared after him, feeling as though she were hovering and being crushed all at once.

'Astrid, you must be very tired. Perhaps we ought to pause for a little rest,' Mrs Wairi said gently.

She pointed to a thatched cottage a couple of bridges away, ivy climbing up its walls, in the centre of a small, densely forested square. 'It's a tea house in the evenings,' she said. 'No one's there just now.'

Astrid raised her chin and followed Mrs Wairi into the tea house. It was quiet in there. Just the sound of the two of them breathing.

She turned and looked at Mrs Wairi.

Later, Astrid would try her best to forget about what came next. It was embarrassing to look back: shameful. The howling, the sobs, the way she had punched and kicked Mrs Wairi, the accusations she had hurled at her. She had begged to go back to her mother, screamed until her throat was hoarse, threatened to flee, sworn that she would reveal London Overhead to the world, sworn that she didn't want wings, didn't want anything, except to go home.

Mrs Wairi sat with her. She didn't defend herself when Astrid hit her. And when, at last, Astrid sagged down in exhaustion on the velvet settee, Mrs Wairi stayed with her.

'It's better than the rhubarb shed,' she heard Mrs Wairi say quietly, and Astrid wasn't sure whether she was comforting Astrid or herself.

Astrid curled into a tight ball. Mama was weeping, far away. And it was her fault.

She had chosen to leave.

It didn't matter that Mama had locked her up. Astrid loved her. And she had rejected Mama's love. She had sacrificed love for a glimpse of the stars, and found she couldn't even see them.

Alongside the excitement of being in London Overhead, Astrid felt a bone-deep exhaustion. Until now, she had known everything a day would hold. There were no surprises. Her life in the rhubarb shed ticked by like clockwork.

She had no idea what came next. What she would do next, or who she would meet. How her life would unfold.

'I need you to send a message to Mama,' Astrid said, her voice unsteady and hoarse. 'Tell her – tell her I'm safe. Tell her I miss her. Tell her . . . tell her I need her.'

'Of course,' Mrs Wairi said.

'I don't want to stay here,' Astrid whispered. 'I don't want to stay.'

Mrs Wairi said nothing, and moments later, Astrid fell asleep.

* * *

By the time she woke, the sun was low in the sky. Mrs Wairi was standing in the doorway. Silhouetted against the sunset, her wings came forth from her shoulders and fanned out. Every feather was sharp as cut paper.

'Astrid, your mother has been informed that you are safe.'

'I want to go home.'

'No final decisions have been made as yet. I'm willing to discuss your future tomorrow. Agreed?'

Astrid nodded, blinking the sleep from her eyes.

'In the meantime,' Mrs Wairi added, 'I have contacted an optician about your eyesight. She says it ought to improve in the next few days. You might see the stars before you leave us.' She looked around, orange light throwing her features into harsh relief. 'The peak of the Perseids meteor shower is over, of course. But August nights are clear. There's a telescope at the highest point of London Overhead.'

A telescope. Astrid felt a rush of anticipation. She could find all the things she'd read about – the craters and rills on the moon, maybe even the Andromeda Galaxy.

Tomorrow. Mama could wait that long.

'All right,' Astrid said. 'Tomorrow.'

And actually, Astrid reflected as she joined Mrs Wairi outside, the evening sun pleasantly warm on her back, when she returned, she might have a little bargaining power that she'd never had before. Perhaps Mama would consider letting her out at weekends.

A question occurred to her; a question she'd asked before, but still didn't have an answer to. She turned to Mrs Wairi.

'How did you know I was there?'

'Pardon?' Mrs Wairi said.

'In the rhubarb shed. Nobody knew about me except Mama.'

'I'm an acquirer. I studied under the Ceramicists to learn about detection of Librae. You can imagine why. If we're to maintain secrecy, we can't have newly fledged Librae crash-landing all over the world. My job is to read the flight of starlings, interpreting the messages coded in their movements. The Romans called it augury. On the night of Stellfest, when we celebrate the Perseids in London Overhead, I saw a great murmuration pass over London – thousands of starlings. They told me that a child was searching for an escape. A Librae child.'

'Did they tell you where I was?'

'I followed them, and watched for a day. I couldn't act until I was certain that I understood their message correctly.' She smiled. 'Anyway, Astrid, I'd like to get you settled on the Fourth Flower. You remember the boarding house I mentioned?'

It would be filled with children. Astrid had spent her life longing for other children, but now that the reality was presented to her, she felt horribly nervous. What would they think of her?

They set out again, over a glass bridge. There were trees growing down the centre of the bridge, birch saplings with slender green leaves. Their trunks grew directly from the glass, their spreading roots suspended in the clear liquid of a tank below the bridge.

'Do Librae sleep at night or in the day?' Astrid enquired, as a group of teenagers flapped overhead.

'Children sleep during the day, since Starminster is only available to Librae at night,' Mrs Wairi said. 'Everyone else mostly keeps normal hours.'

'So this place is run by the children at night,' Astrid said.

'It isn't, though the children would like to think so,' Mrs Wairi said, smiling wryly. 'Constables patrol in shifts.'

'There are police up here?'

'Certainly. Librae constables.'

A shout from nearby. Councillor Paulson was marching along a wooden bridge adjacent to theirs, waving a phone aggressively at Mrs Wairi. A girl trailed along behind him, clearly buzzing with irritation.

'Using a phone, would you believe!' Councillor Paulson shouted as soon as he was within earshot. 'Appalling behaviour. I'll be speaking to your parents about this, Penelope, just you wait!'

'It's not mine!' the girl protested. 'I literally just *found* the stupid thing and I was *bringing* it to the Second Flower to hand it in. Like a concerned citizen should.'

'Mrs Wairi, a word,' Councillor Paulson snapped, making a swift turn onto the bridge where they stood.

'Goodness, Councillor, I'm in rather a rush. I need to get Astrid to the Fourth Flower before my meeting. Can't you manage a rogue phone yourself?'

'You know very well, Mrs Wairi, that a *rogue phone* is a threat to London Overhead's security.'

'Not with the safeguards the Ceramicists have enacted,' Mrs Wairi muttered.

'Anyway,' Councillor Paulson added, 'it's not just about the phone. It's about what's on the screen.'

The girl looked over at Astrid, and her mouth fell open.

Mrs Wairi took the phone. Her grip tightened as she looked at the phone's screen, scrolling with her thumb. 'Right,' she said. 'I'll hold onto this, Penelope.'

'It's not mine!' the girl said again.

'I can't spare any more time,' Mrs Wairi said. 'You'll take Astrid to the Fourth Flower, Councillor, won't you?'

She didn't wait for a reply. Her wings flared open, and Mrs Wairi took off. A breeze streamed over Astrid's face as Mrs Wairi sped away, soon lost among the buildings of the city below.

'You're not busy, Penelope. You wouldn't mind showing Astrid the way, I'm sure,' Councillor Paulson said quickly, his own wings appearing.

A moment later, he was gone as well, leaving Astrid standing on the bridge with the girl.

7

The two girls were exactly the same height.

Astrid smiled tentatively at the girl. Penelope had brown skin where Astrid's was starkly pale. Her hair was black as a crow's wing, and Astrid's was white-blonde. Her face was dimpled and cheery. Astrid knew that she looked solemn, with a thin face and a permanent crease between her eyebrows.

But Penelope was still a child. Just like her.

As soon as Councillor Paulson was out of sight, Penelope burst out, 'Did they bring you here?'

'What?'

'The phone,' Penelope said, 'it had a news story about *you*. I was reading it when Councillor Nosy Parker Paulson came

57

prancing along. It said you were missing from your mum's house.' She shook her head, long braid flying. 'You're, like, BBC homepage material.'

Mama had reported Astrid's disappearance to the police. But surely there would be questions galore. After all, no one but Mama even knew that Astrid existed.

She was risking serious trouble. She must be *desperate* to get Astrid back home.

'It's fine,' Astrid said. 'I'm not staying.'

'Not staying where?'

'Here,' Astrid said. 'London Overhead.'

The girl leaned forward. 'Why? This is the best place in the world. Even when you're not fledged. You're not, are you?'

'No. Are you?'

'Nope.' The girl smiled. The smile transformed her face – her eyes, her forehead, her cheeks, everything seemed to twinkle and beam with mischief and delight. 'I'm Penelope. Pent for short. And you're Astrid, right?'

Astrid nodded. 'Why was the phone such a big deal?'

The smile vanished. 'Secrecy, and all that. Phones are a disaster up here. Nothing's secure, from pictures to GPS. I had every safeguard on it that I could figure out, but the Overlords don't know the first thing about technology, so they won't appreciate my skills. Although maybe if I'm lucky, your cameo on the BBC might distract from my rule breaking.'

'I thought you said the phone wasn't yours.'

'Obviously, I said that. Unfortunately, the wallpaper is literally a selfie, so I suspect trouble is coming my way. My parents haven't even got a teensy-weensy sense of humour about rule breaking. Whoops. Anyway. Enough about me. You're supposed to be going to the Fourth Flower?'

'Don't you live there, as well?' Astrid asked.

'No. My parents are Librae too. We live in a nesthome. Which has its pros and cons. There won't be anyone at the Fourth Flower now. Lessons are beginning shortly. Let's go to Starminster instead.'

Astrid looked over at the dome. The last hint of sunlight outlined it in gold. She felt a tug towards the building, proudly ancient and ornate amongst the glassy skyscrapers.

'Okay,' Astrid said, and they started walking.

'So you're going to live on the Fourth Flower, are you? My friend Mason lives there. He's actually the most hilarious person I know. Not that I ever see him these days. He skives lessons all the time.'

'I'm not staying, like I said,' Astrid said. 'I'm going home tomorrow.'

'What about when you fledge?'

'Why would fledging make a difference?'

'You can't just take to the skies when you get wings,' Pent said. 'You need to learn how to fly. That's what Starminster teaches.'

'But birds can fly pretty much straight away.'

'We're not birds. It takes a while to learn to use our wings. I might ask Mr Barker about it. He teaches Librae history. I could happily listen to him burble away all day.'

'Do you learn normal subjects at Starminster? Like maths, and all that?'

'Oh, yes. You'd not get far anywhere else if you didn't, and lots of Librae have normal jobs. But there's plenty of lessons that are focused on flying. Aeronautical physics, thermodynamics, that sort of thing. There're practical lessons, too, but obviously we can only watch them.'

Astrid thought of her home-schooling curriculum, with its strict diet of literature and mathematics and science. Always the same. The teacher onscreen; the modelling of tasks; the practice exercises. This would be entirely different, and better still, she'd be surrounded by others. Maybe even friends.

That is, if she was planning to stay. Which she wasn't.

They went down the moss-covered stairs Astrid remembered from yesterday and stepped onto the gallery that wrapped around the exterior of the dome. 'This is the Stone Gallery,' Pent said, pushing open a door.

It was quieter inside, with the distracting wind hushed. At the bottom of a long spiral of stairs, they walked out into the cathedral.

Astrid stopped, catching her breath.

Not a stone in the cathedral was left unadorned: embellished with gold, with mosaics, with painting, with gleaming polished wood. Astrid couldn't stop staring. She felt that she could stare at St Paul's Cathedral for years, and still be surprised by some unseen detail.

All was golden, like the rhubarb shed, but the rhubarb shed turned gigantic, extravagant in every detail, filled up with light like a glass of water, even now that the sun had gone down.

'I like it,' Astrid said quietly.

'Me, too,' Pent said. 'I come here a lot. I can't wait until I can . . .' She stretched out her arms. 'I just want to fly through this place, you know?'

Astrid nodded. She wanted to open her wings and fly up into the domed ceiling that baffled and bewildered the eye, to see the statues and images up close.

As they walked over the black and white tiles, Astrid noticed that one of the vast pillars had a piece of paper taped to it.

The words on the paper snagged at her eye, all in capital letters: MISSING CHILD.

She stopped.

A photograph of a paper-white child, thin and insubstantial, with dark eyes and no hint of a smile. The background was blurred, but Astrid could smell the fresh earth. It could only be the rhubarb shed.

Below, it said, HAVE YOU SEEN ASTRID CROSSLEY? MISSING FROM HER HOME SINCE 18TH AUGUST.

Pent, standing behind her, said, 'Wow. The police in London Underfoot are quick workers, aren't they?'

Astrid unpeeled the tape and folded the poster in half, shoving it into her pocket. 'I'll be home tomorrow.'

'History's starting shortly,' Pent said, looking at her watch. 'Most of the theory lessons are down in the crypt.'

Pent led on. The crypt was bracketed with pillars, its ceiling of vaulted stone. They passed statues and memorials and iron gates like blackened teeth. The buzz of conversation echoed from up ahead.

'As a person of Pakistani heritage, I'm mortified that I have to say these words out loud,' Pent said, 'but this is the Chapel of the Order of the British Empire.'

About thirty children sat in the chapel, half on the chairs

and half on the floor. Pent sat down cross-legged on the stone floor and gestured for Astrid to join her.

'There are plenty of free chairs,' Astrid whispered.

'We don't get one until we fledge.'

So the children in the chairs had fledged. Most of them looked a little older. They wore pale grey jackets with slits in the back.

Astrid closed her eyes for a second and felt dizzy. All those faces, all the thoughts behind them.

The teacher came in, only his white hair visible over a messy pile of notes he was carrying, which he dumped on a nearby altar. Half of them slid off.

'That's Mr Barker,' Pent whispered.

'Evening,' he said. Immediately, the conversation stopped. 'Today's question. Ask anything about Librae history, and I will endeavour to answer.'

A boy raised his hand. He was sitting on the floor. Unfledged.

'Fred Moutts,' Mr Barker said.

'How did London Overhead get water?'

'A fine question,' Mr Barker said. 'At present, we have a borehole and our own sewerage system, constructed in Victorian times. The tunnels are small and concealed with Ceramicist enchantments. Before that, however, the city was reliant entirely on rainfall, which led to one of our most important festivals. Rick, its name?'

A boy with intelligent eyes looked up. 'Rain Muster,' he said.

'Correct. It's ceremonial now, but Rain Muster was once essential. Obviously, we now are in a period of climate change, which impacts weather patterns, but they were a little more consistent back then. Often by the end of summer, water was scarce. When the first great storm of the autumn came, the Librae brought out vessels of every type to catch the water – pails, teacups, vases, chamber pots. The rainwater was emptied into their nesthome's cistern. It was a matter of survival.'

'Why couldn't they carry water up from London Underfoot?' someone asked.

'Access was more difficult then. The Ceramicists' enchantments were rudimentary, and one could only access the city via Starminster. Numbers of Librae entering and leaving the city were strictly controlled for reasons of secrecy.'

'How did Rain Muster become an art exhibition, then?' a girl said.

Mr Barker smiled. 'Ah, the corruption of history! It started with a competition. Who could design a container capable of catching and retaining the most rainwater? Think of your physics, students. What kind of container might win?'

Fred raised his hand. 'Something with a large surface area,' he said, 'connecting to a storage bottle below.'

'Precisely,' Mr Barker said. 'You've got an engineering mind, Fred. Then the competition evolved, becoming a matter of aesthetics – of beauty. We now hold an art exhibition on the top tier of the Hanging Gardens. The main requirement is that water is used in an innovative way. Last year, for example, I recall musical instruments that chimed as rain fell; a tiny glass train that carried water from tank to tank; a fountain of oiled silk umbrellas.'

'Two questions,' said a girl. 'Why are so many of the exhibits made of silver? And why do we sing?'

'Superstition, in part. Rainsong, to raise the rain, to encourage the clouds to shed their weight. Silver was believed to purify the water. But above all, Rain Muster is a festival – we come together, we sing, we appreciate what is beautiful. Such celebrations make our lives worthwhile. Consider Stellfest, a few nights ago, when we pay tribute to the stars and their gift to us in the light of the Perseids. And it's not long until the Month of Birthdays, either.'

Rain Muster, thought Astrid. *Stellfest. The Month of Birthdays.* It surprised her to think that Librae might have their own festivals. She wondered what they involved, what rituals or gifts or decorations. It would be fascinating to see how the Librae celebrated.

Mr Barker went on. 'This year, we expect Rain Muster in about three weeks, depending on the forecast. I look forward to celebrating it with you.'

He paused. 'Notebooks out, everyone. Write down, in brief, the answer to Fred's question.'

Mr Barker circulated the class, pausing next to Astrid.

'You're a newcomer?' he said, giving her a notebook and pencil.

Astrid nodded.

'I thought so,' he said. 'You've got that slightly overwhelmed look. It's a lot, isn't it?'

'I'm not staying,' Astrid said.

'No?'

'I'm leaving tomorrow.'

'Better make good notes, then,' Mr Barker said, not unkindly. He returned to the front of the classroom as Astrid scribbled down a few sentences.

She'd read about Victorian sewers, the lost rivers that flowed beneath the city. But this was completely different. Suddenly, she had a thousand questions. How was London Overhead built, and by whom? Who constructed the flowers, and how did they manage that in secret? What about the other Librae settlements Mrs Wairi had mentioned? What about the sky forests?

If she stayed, a little voice in her mind told her, she could ask. She'd have her own ticket to the secrets of the Librae world.

'One final question,' Mr Barker said later. 'Anyone?'

Astrid slowly lifted her hand. It would be her last chance to ask a question, so she might as well seize the opportunity. There was something else that Mrs Wairi had said that she still didn't understand.

'Yes?'

'Why are we called Librae? Is it to do with the zodiac?'

She flushed suddenly, remembering Mrs Wairi's condescension at the mention of the zodiac term Libra, but Mr Barker was nodding enthusiastically.

'An excellent question,' he said, 'and one all students ought to be able to answer. Librae must be born within the dates of the twenty-third of September and the twenty-third of October. Does this mean, however, that everyone born in this bracket will one day fledge? Penelope?'

'No,' Pent said. 'But your chances are greater if your parents are Librae too.'

'How close the ancients came to discovering our secret,' Mr Barker said. 'The mystical rubbed cheek-to-cheek with scientific phenomena, and they had no way of discerning which they had witnessed. They knew that the constellation Libra was an air sign; they knew the dates; they even knew of the Libran concept of balance, the understanding that we have that we are both human and bird, both earth and sky, dwelling always in the in-between. Yet they missed the reality: that some Libras will fledge and become Librae. And some will not.'

'Does that mean there are other zodiac signs?' Rick asked. 'Real ones – like us?'

'Perhaps there were, once,' Mr Barker said. 'Who can know? But no longer.'

Again, they were instructed to take notes. A bell rang fifteen minutes later, and the students departed a few at a time. Pent kept up a quiet running commentary as they went.

'That's Claudette Windsor, rich as the royals, eider duck wings. Quite striking, black and white. Anton Borg, buzzard. Faster than you'd believe. Christa Summerling. Canada goose. Meh, in my opinion. Massive wingspan, though.'

'Does the bird's species make a difference?'

'Yep,' Pent said. 'Librae fly much faster than birds, because our wings are bigger, but speed still depends on your species. Oscar, with the mullet, he's got the wings of a Eurasian woodcock.' She lowered her voice to a whisper. 'One of the slowest flying birds. But once Oscar gets going, he can motor along at twenty-seven, twenty-eight miles per hour. Which still puts him behind everyone else, but it's not bad.'

'Does it matter what kind of wings you have?' Astrid asked.

Pent climbed to her feet, stretching. The other unfledged students were moving into yoga poses, or grimacing.

'Matter?' Pent said. 'I mean – it shouldn't, right? It's not like it makes any difference to who we are.'

Astrid nodded, closing her notebook and tucking it into the waistband of her pyjamas. She'd forgotten she was still wearing them. Her eyes prickled again. Mama had patched a hole in one of the knees.

'It matters,' Pent said. 'Yep. For whatever reason, it matters. Anyway, given that we're nocturnal, it's both lunchtime and midnight now. D'you want to get some food? There's a canteen at the other end of the crypt. Though I've got a packed lunch. Don't know how you feel about paneer, but you're welcome to share . . .'

'Actually,' Astrid said, 'there's something I have to do first.'

* * *

When Pent heard Astrid's plan, she offered to take her back upstairs and they set off.

'Have a look at this,' Pent said, stopping at a door halfway up the spiral stairs of the cathedral.

They stood on a narrow walkway that stretched around the whole interior of the dome. The ceiling was a kaleidoscope, honeycombed with golden tiles and entangled with vines.

There were angels everywhere: stone angels, golden mosaic angels, painted angels, their wings extended.

'This is the Whispering Gallery,' Pent said. Her voice sounded different, colliding with the surfaces and coming at Astrid from all directions. 'Lots of the practical lessons happen up here.'

Astrid peered over the railing. Candles burned along the choir stalls. They shone like lost stars, the golden candlelight softly familiar to Astrid's tired eyes.

For a moment, she could almost hear the rhubarb, the small gunshots of its growth.

Then the imagined rhubarb was drowned out by raised voices from below.

'I won't have that girl here, Kalekye. You were not clear with me about the circumstances of her acquisition. She should never have been brought to London Overhead.'

Astrid peered over the edge and saw Mrs Wairi and the Headmaster. Mrs Wairi was speaking, but they could only hear snatches.

70

'. . . Paulson went down to Lye . . . there were further reinforcements on the shed. No intention . . .'

'Irrelevant,' Mr Finifugal said. 'The mother won't give up. She'll do whatever it takes to get her daughter back.'

'Nonsense,' Mrs Wairi snapped. 'It will blow over.'

They moved out of sight. Pent was looking at Astrid, mouth open.

'Your mum really wants you home,' she said.

They went back through the door and climbed more stairs, then came out into the cool air of the Stone Gallery.

'The night's clear, right?' Pent said. 'But look at the light pollution.'

The city below twinkled feverishly, like spilled treasure. A fug rose from London Underfoot, every droplet of water, every particle of car exhaust, catching and refracting the light until the sky was a blur of artificial luminescence.

'The highest point of London Overhead is the Crow's Nest. It's nearly half a mile up and it's got a telescope,' Pent said. 'But it takes ages to get there. And Thermodynamics starts at one a.m., so you'll be on your own.'

'That's fine.'

Pent drew a sketchy map in her notebook, then tore it out and gave it to Astrid. 'I guess if you're leaving tomorrow, this is goodbye,' she said. 'Good luck!' She waved, and disappeared back inside.

Tomorrow, this strange dream would be over, Astrid thought, and she would be safe again in the rhubarb shed.

And never see Pent again, never experience the stirring of new friendship, a voice said, and Astrid pushed it away.

She started her journey on a wooden bridge that swayed beneath every step, then turned onto a spiral staircase. Its crimson paint flaked off on the palms of her hands as she walked up. It went on for so long, around and around, that she became dizzy, and when she finally arrived on a grassy platform, she stopped to recover and check Pent's map.

From there, she followed a stone bridge across several small meadow-squares, passing the foxglove, which Pent had marked as 'Flower 8' on her map. Then it was staircases again; creaky wooden ones, a few slippery marble steps, one that took her around three sides of a dark-windowed skyscraper, her own face looking back at her.

Her legs burned from the exertion. But the light from below was less intrusive, and she could finally see a single platform above everything else, a rope ladder swinging below.

When Astrid came to it and took hold of the rungs, it shuddered in the wind.

At the top, the telescope was spindly against the sky. Astrid knelt to catch her breath, then looked up.

It took her eyes a moment to focus.

The stars.

Pinpricks of light. Silvery, faint.

Compared to the dazzle of the city below, the stars were indistinct. They didn't blaze. But seeing them herself, in real life – wonder expanded within her. Astrid's eyes filled with tears of joy.

They were more beautiful than she had imagined. And better, they were familiar. There were the Pleiades, there was Orion's belt. Pegasus! Mars, faintly pink and steady.

She examined the stars through the telescope. It took a while to figure out how it worked, but once she could adjust the focus, she found she could see Venus, too.

Seeing them, Astrid understood why people believed that stars could prophesy the twists and turns of a life.

Soon she would be separated from them again.

Astrid moved away from the telescope, eyes wandering the sky, visiting other worlds. She leaned against the sturdy wooden railing.

Her fingers traced the wood absently as she stared up. Someone had been at it with a knife.

Astrid glanced down. The carving was difficult to make out in the darkness. Two letters.

Initials.

It can't be.

But there it was.

EC.

Surely it couldn't be Erika Crossley. It must be another person with the same initials. It couldn't be Mama.

Or could it?

The 'E' – it was just as Mama had taught her to write it. A crescent, and a line crossing it.

Mama had stood here. She knew about London Overhead.

Was she a Librae too? But Mama's birthday was in November. Unless she had lied . . .

But – what if Mama knew that Astrid was a Librae? What if that was the reason that Mama had kept her in the shed her whole life? To prevent her from finding out; to stop her from leaving home to attend Starminster?

But why? What could possibly be harmful about fledging? Why wouldn't Mama want Astrid to live in this beautiful city, to be a Librae? If Mama knew, then surely she'd see sense – she'd want Astrid to possess the sky.

74

Then she remembered Mrs Wairi's words, clear as if she was hearing them for the first time.

Paulson went down to Lye . . . there were further reinforcements on the shed. No intention . . .

No intention of letting Astrid out.

Mama had made further reinforcements on the shed. So that Astrid could never escape again.

Tomorrow she could be back home, in the rhubarb shed, where every day repeated the same comforting routine as the day before. Where she'd be safe; where she'd be a prisoner.

Or she could stay up here. She could have friends. She could have wings.

She could belong.

She heard wingbeats.

It was Mrs Wairi. As she landed, her wings caught the light from below, iridescent, gleaming like oil. 'I was looking for you,' she said. 'I didn't expect to find you so far up.'

Astrid smiled at Mrs Wairi, the light of the stars all around them. Moments of regret might come later – for now, she felt only elation.

Both Londons glittered below.

'I've changed my mind,' she said. 'I've decided to stay.'

8

Mrs Wairi walked Astrid to the Fourth Flower. It was slow going; Astrid's feet ached. Below, the sinuous train rails sparked like lightning.

On the way, Mrs Wairi said delicately, 'Perhaps you would like to shower?'

'Yes, please,' Astrid said.

Mrs Wairi showed Astrid to a silver dome that sat in the centre of a platform.

'It's a communal bathroom,' Mrs Wairi said. 'Nesthomes rarely have reliable plumbing. It's got showers, baths, toilets – everything you could need. Take your time. I'll bring you clean clothes.'

Inside, there was a hallway with many glowing buttons, some red, some green.

Astrid pressed a green button. A door opened. She went inside, the door sliding shut behind her.

Despite the steely exterior, the inside looked as if it had formed over a couple of millennia. A pool of natural stone steamed gently, and around the edges, plants gleamed vividly green. At the edge of the pool, a small waterfall tinkled.

Astrid shed her pyjamas and dipped her toes into the water. It was deliciously warm.

She waded in, feeling her muscles relax. The stone beneath her skin was satin smooth. A little exploration led her to glass bottles standing on the side. Astrid washed her hair with eucalyptus-scented shampoo and rinsed it in the waterfall. Bubbles gathered around her like white lace.

A soft chime. A basket slid out of the wall.

Astrid soaked for a little longer, then got out to investigate the basket, which bore a fluffy white towel, a backpack including a toothbrush and hairbrush, plimsolls, a pair of black leggings and a striped T-shirt.

She dried off and dressed, then brushed her teeth and hair. The threadbare pyjamas were stowed away in the backpack.

Mrs Wairi stood outside.

'It's lovely in there. How come Librae have such nice things?'

'Wealth,' Mrs Wairi said. 'Librae pay high taxes to live here, and the Overlords spend lavishly on utilities. They try to bring the beauty of the natural world into London Overhead.'

The sun was rising, its light diffused and gentle. Astrid had already been in the city for almost twenty-four hours. She stared up at the bustling sky, filled with Librae.

'Are the Overlords like the king?' she asked.

'More like Parliament. Councillor Paulson is an Overlord. Do you know much about politics?'

'Not really,' Astrid said vaguely. 'Mama never has anything good to say about politics, so she rarely talks about it.'

'Your mother would probably fit right in here, then,' Mrs Wairi said, with a tense smile. 'Politics are . . . a minefield.'

'Mrs Wairi,' Astrid said slowly. 'Did you ever know someone called Erika Crossley?'

A momentary pause, then Mrs Wairi shook her head. 'That's your mother's name, isn't it?'

'She was here,' Astrid said, abandoning pretence.

'It's unlikely, Astrid.'

'She was. I know it. Her initials . . . they're carved up there, at the Crow's Nest.'

'There are lots of people with those initials,' Mrs Wairi said. 'Come on. Let's get to the Fourth Flower.'

The Fourth Flower was a giant buttercup. They walked

through the wide double doors, and collided with a wave of sound. Laughter and shrieks of joy.

'All of our externals live here – about a hundred in all.'

A swimming pool glittered in the centre of the buttercup, which was open to the skies like the Shard had been. Children splashed in it, and a caustic smell came at Astrid in warm moist waves.

'The swimming pool's useful for training,' Mrs Wairi said. 'Helps develop your muscles for when you fledge. Everything else is just for fun.'

The pool resembled the bathroom, with stony river-like slides shooting shrieking children out into the water. Hibiscus trees, bright with flowers, shadowed the pool's edges.

Overhead, ziplines hung between the buttercup's petals, and older children were playing on them, swinging and somersaulting and catching themselves. There was an enormous trampoline, like a mezzanine, overhead, children bouncing and launching themselves into the sky, to open their wings or to plunge into the swimming pool with great splashes.

Enormous tubes twined around the inside of the petals, painted the colours of the rainbow.

'What are those?' Astrid asked.

'Convenience slides. Some of them lead to transition points in London Underfoot, though I wouldn't recommend that you head there at present, given the search for you. A few of the slides take you to other parts of London Overhead. Do note the red one, which is for emergencies. It will take you directly to St Thomas' Accident and Emergency.'

Astrid couldn't stop herself from smiling. She wanted to try out that trampoline, to splash in that pool. Maybe Pent would come to visit.

'Here's a key to a sleeping pod, Astrid. Number fourteen. Those transparent bubbles. I'm told you can see the sky. You might be able to make out a star or two.'

She held out the key and Astrid took it.

'I'll see you at some point. I'm needed on the ground now.'

'Will you be back soon?'

'Perhaps. But I have responsibilities in London Underfoot.' Mrs Wairi patted her on the shoulder. 'You've made the right choice, Astrid.'

She flew upwards, through the open petals of the buttercup. A few of the children waved up at Mrs Wairi as she disappeared. She'd probably brought them here, like Astrid.

Astrid headed towards the cluster of pods and found number fourteen. She fumbled with the key until she managed to twist it, wrist aching. Frustrating, the way she'd never learned these basic skills.

She went inside, pressing the buttons next to the door until she succeeded in darkening the transparent walls and turning on the light. It illuminated a low bed with a puffy duvet, a wardrobe, and in a door, a tiny cubicle with a sink, shower and toilet.

She went to the sink and washed her face in the freezing water that came out of the tap. Then she put her head under the tap and drank until her mouth was no longer dry.

Her stomach rumbled. She still hadn't eaten. How long had it been since she'd left the shed? Time was passing like falling syrup, slowly, then in a great dollop.

Astrid lay down on the bed, which felt incomparably soft.

Outside, a great wave of laughter. Tomorrow, she might join in.

But another part of her still longed for Mama and the rhubarb shed. She took out the old pyjamas from her backpack and buried her face in the familiar scent of the shed and Mama as she fell asleep.

*   *   *

When Astrid woke, it took a moment to remember where she was. It was quiet. The clock on the wall reported that that it was nine in the evening.

81

The Fourth Flower was quiet, the swimming pool still. Everyone must be at Starminster.

She pushed the double doors open.

Below, the lights of London Underfoot were turning on, a few at a time. The sky was clear and greenish, loose skeins of cloud moving ponderously. The tropical wings of a Librae on a low flightpath caught the light, throwing out flares of jade-green as she flew.

It looked easy. Graceful. Pent had said it wasn't, but Astrid would work as hard as it took to fly like a bird. The beauty of the place at sundown thrilled her, and her hope grew. The city belonged to her.

It was her future.

Many of the skyscrapers sparkled, and Starminster looked almost dowdy among them. Even a century ago, Astrid thought, it must have commanded the cityscape of both Londons. It must have been the tallest building you could imagine. Apart from the flowers, of course. If they were also there a century ago.

That would be her next question for Mr Barker, if she dared raise her hand again. Who built the flowers? What was their purpose? Why was the weird, alien-looking flower the highest one of all?

Astrid set out towards Starminster. With her destination visible, navigating London Overhead ought to have been easy, but she was beginning to discover that many of the staircases and bridges were unsafe. A few had warning signs attached, but others were more subtly treacherous, missing railings or planks.

Astrid had to turn back several times. Eventually, she pulled out the notebook from yesterday and began to write down directions, crossing out her failed efforts.

4th Flower to Starminster: Rusty bridge, left onto rickety staircase (skip step 5 dodgy), short blue bridge towards turret (v slippery!!).

A divide was emerging between parts of London Overhead: the luxurious flowers, the lovingly designed bathrooms – and the crumbling bridges and stairs. Somehow, it reminded her of the wingless students, sitting in a row on the floor.

9

When Astrid reached Starminster, she passed a group of older children standing on the Stone Gallery. They were grooming one another's wings and chatting. One after the other, the group took off, still calling to one another. A feather fell from one enormous wing.

Astrid's eyes were on the feather. She had an odd urge to touch it and see if it was as soft as it looked. But as it drifted towards the net, then slipped through it, the feather disappeared.

Astrid rubbed her eyes. What on earth? Was this some sort of bizarre by-product of hunger? Had she developed malnutrition overnight or something?

As she was staring, mystified, at the net, a voice called her name.

'Astrid!'

It was Pent. She was smiling. 'What are you doing back here? I thought you'd headed home.'

'Yeah,' Astrid said. 'I sort of . . . decided against it, after all.'

'Good call. I had a feeling you might do that. And it's your lucky day, because Mum made croissants and I happen to have a few spares.' She held out a napkin. 'Why're you staring at the ground like it stole your mother?' She paused, then said, reddening, 'Sorry. That was the stupidest thing I could possibly say. I really am sorry.'

'Don't worry,' Astrid said. She accepted the napkin. The croissants were still warm, and she sank her teeth into the flaky pastry. 'Thanks so much,' she said through mouthfuls. 'I have a weird question. Please don't think I'm losing my mind, but a feather dropped from someone's wings and vanished.'

Pent laughed. 'You're not losing your mind. You know the Ceramicists?'

'Everyone keeps mentioning them, but no.'

Pent nodded. 'The Ceramicists keep London Overhead hidden. But it's not just invisible. It's not real at all for the Underfooters.'

'I don't understand.'

'Neither do I, not really,' Pent said. 'Basically, to those living

85

on the ground, London Overhead isn't just impossible to see – it doesn't exist. So low-flying aircraft and drones can't touch the city or the Librae. It's actually quite creepy to see a plane passing through you, like a ghost. You can see London Overhead, and you can see people flying in the sky within its borders, because you washed your eyes with the mud, right?'

'Right,' Astrid said through a mouthful of flaky croissant. 'But . . . I still don't get the feather thing.'

'It's because a feather's part of us,' Pent said. 'Or maybe I should say part of a fledged Librae, since everyone's always reminding us how unfledged and insignificant *we* are. A massive feather like that could cause questions if an Underfooter found it, so once it reaches the level of that huge silvery net you've probably seen by now, it's – it's just gone.'

It made a reluctant kind of sense. 'Where does it go?'

'Who knows? I sometimes imagine the Ceramicists have a little room somewhere that's full of Librae feathers. Maybe they stuff their pillows with them.'

Astrid mulled on this. 'So . . . what *are* the Ceramicists?'

'People. I assume. Never seen one. Apparently, they live in the First Flower – that big weird-looking one in the centre of London Overhead.'

'Are they Librae?'

'It's all a big huge massive *secret,* so who knows?' Pent wiggled her hands dramatically. 'Do you think it only works for feathers? Because I've occasionally wondered, if I *really* needed the loo . . .'

Astrid laughed, imagining a stream of urine fizzling into nonexistence.

'Did you walk here?' Pent asked. 'You could have taken the indigo slide, you know.'

'I've never been down a slide.'

Pent's eyebrows leapt. 'Are you serious? How have you managed to get through your entire childhood without going down a slide? I know we have lots of them up here, but there are slides everywhere. Playgrounds, hello?'

Astrid opened her mouth, then closed it.

Pent nodded wisely. 'Overprotective parents. Although clearly not overprotective enough, given that Mrs Wairi was able to take you.' She put her hands over her mouth. 'I'm so sorry. I'm not flexible enough to literally put my foot in my mouth, but I . . . I never think before I speak. And I know it's not on.'

Astrid wanted to reply, but couldn't think of a single word to say. She finished eating her croissants.

Pent also lapsed into silence for a moment, before bursting out with, 'Now you're cross with me.'

'I'm not cross,' Astrid said. 'It isn't like you said anything that's not true.'

'Mum says I'm insensitive.'

'There are worse things. Better to be insensitive than a liar.' Astrid remembered the initials carved into the Crow's Nest, and that faraway look Mama used to get. Was Astrid right? Had Mama lived here once a upon a time? Had she been missing London Overhead?

She put Mama out of her mind determinedly.

'Do we have a lesson to get to, then?'

'Yep,' said Pent. 'Morality and Ethics. Mr Strangley's the teacher, but he's been off since the start of term earlier this month, so it's our first lesson with him.'

At least there'd be one subject where she wouldn't be weeks behind all the other pupils, Astrid thought. 'Doesn't the school year start in September?'

'We'll be off for Rain Muster, so tragically they cut our summer short in cruel retaliation. Let's go.'

Astrid and Pent set off down the stairs. Other students were coming up, and one girl was flying, her white wings widespread. She nearly knocked them over, but didn't pause to apologise.

'That's Beatrix,' Pent said. 'She's older than us, obviously. There are three classes at Starminster, though it's dependent on ability, not age. Fledglings – our group, though we haven't fledged – is all the beginners. Then there's Lower Flights, sort of intermediate, and Upper Flights. Beatrix is in Upper Flights. She's Head Girl.'

When they reached St Dunstan's Chapel, near the imposing front door of the cathedral, Astrid sat obediently on the floor with the other unfledged students. The chapel was lit with candles. The glow felt warm on Astrid's face, familiar.

When Mr Strangley arrived, the students hushed instantly. He stood in the entrance, sweeping the students' faces with dark, intense eyes. He lingered on Astrid's face for a second.

'Good evening,' he said at last, going to the front. Unlike Mr Barker, he had no papers. He sat down on the altar, wrinkling its white cloth.

'I passed a lesson by Mr Barker on my way here,' he said. 'Experienced teacher. Runs his lessons as a Q&A, I believe. The students seem to enjoy it.'

Astrid glanced around. Everyone was focused on Mr Strangley. His accent was Irish, she thought, harsh and lilting at the same time.

'I'm not answering your questions,' Mr Strangley said, leaning forward. 'I'm more interested in asking *you* a few questions. I don't want you listening. I want you thinking.'

Astrid sensed the tension rising – postures straightening, a few students looking determinedly elsewhere.

'What is the title of this course?' Mr Strangley said, pointing at a boy in the front row.

'Morality and Ethics,' the boy said.

'Correct,' Mr Strangley said. 'What does that mean?' He looked around, his gaze sharp. 'You,' he said, pointing at Pent. 'What do you expect to be taught in this course?'

Astrid could feel Pent's temperature rising. She twisted her fingers nervously. 'How to – how to behave?'

Mr Strangley laughed, and the tension dissipated. It was a laugh that rolled freely, deep and slow and powerful as a river. A laugh that included everyone; a laugh that did not mock Pent for her answer, but instead invited the class to participate in a joke they had yet to understand.

'No. That's not my responsibility. Now, before I begin to help you to open your minds, I will stop one custom that is complete poppycock.' He paused. 'If you're unfledged, stand up.'

Astrid and the others got to their feet. The rustle of their movement echoed in the small space, and the candle flames dipped.

'Take a seat,' Mr Strangley said.

Astrid glanced at Pent sidelong.

'You, blonde girl,' Mr Strangley said, pointing at Astrid, 'no need to get permission from your friend. Sit down. Sit wherever you like. You're not a second-class citizen of London Overhead. You're not a lady-in-waiting. You're not on the brink of becoming valuable, becoming a person. No one was invited here by accident. You're students of Starminster, every one of you. Wings or no wings, you'll all sit in my lessons.'

For a moment, no one moved.

'Now!'

They hurried into chairs.

'So here's a question for you, to start you off. I want you to think, students. I don't want you passively accepting what I tell you, or what Mr Barker tells you, or any of the other teachers. I want you to think about *why* unfledged students have been told to sit on the floor. How is that supposed to make you feel, whether you're fledged or not? Whose idea was it? And who benefits from your inequality?'

His gaze skimmed over them again, forceful and incisive.

'Here endeth the lesson,' he said, and walked away, his wings unfolding as he went. He took off at the end of the chapel, leaving the class gaping after him.

10

Pent dug a gleeful elbow into Astrid's side. Astrid doubled over.

'Oh, sorry – was that a bit hard?' Pent said. 'I like him. Short, sweet, revolutionary. Exactly right for a lesson. You know what? We should refuse to sit on the floor any more.'

'I'm not exactly the rule-breaking type,' Astrid muttered, rubbing her ribs. 'I know you just live for an illicit phone, etcetera, but I'm more head-down-do-as-I'm-told.'

'And Strangley knew that, didn't he? He absolutely picked up on your nervousness. He's right. We *shouldn't* be sitting on the floor.'

'What did he pick up from you?'

'Probably that I thought Morality and Ethics was an incredibly wishy-washy name for a subject.'

Pent got up and slung her backpack over one shoulder, leaving the chapel with the others, all talking excitedly amongst themselves. The fledged students were looking over at the unfledged ones, as if already calculating the competition for chairs.

'What lesson have we got next?'

'Aerodynamics. No mind-openings there, just hard graft and non-stop calculations. Dr Postlethwaite doesn't mess around.'

Aerodynamics took place in All Souls' Chapel. Dr Postlethwaite soon arrived, wheeling a portable whiteboard.

The unfledged students shuffled their feet a little as the fledged ones took their seats. Astrid saw Fred take a step towards a chair. But then two students who had been conferring in whispers sat firmly on the floor, backs against the wall, and the other unfledged students followed suit, including a reluctant Pent. It seemed like the revolution wasn't going to happen today.

Astrid got out her notebook and began to copy down the complex calculations that Dr Postlethwaite was scribbling, at speed, on the whiteboard.

Dr Postlethwaite was explaining air resistance and its impact on Librae flight. 'It's a form of friction, essentially, the air pulling against the body. So when you are flying, what are some ways you can reduce air resistance?'

The students looked surreptitiously at one another, keeping their heads down.

'Come on, now,' Dr Postlethwaite said. 'Nobody? Deborah? Gregory?'

Two heads shook.

Astrid remembered her lessons at home, her brief flare of fascination with physics. Hesitantly, she lifted her hand. 'Is it . . . making your body more streamlined?'

'Precisely,' he said. 'Since the rest of you are looking utterly at sea, let's go out into the transept for a practical demonstration.'

The students followed.

'Observe as I fly down the nave,' he ordered.

He deployed his wings, which were black and white, polka-dotted. 'He's got common loon wings. Suits him,' Pent whispered with a giggle.

He stretched out his arms, took off and flapped down the nave of the cathedral and back again.

'Note my shape,' he said, slightly out of breath, when he landed. 'Arms out at right angles to the body can make one feel more stable, but in fact it has the opposite effect, because of air resistance – pay attention, Oliver. I allowed my legs to hang down, which is a common mistake you'll see in novice Librae; again, drag will make you uncomfortable, unbalanced and slow. It's a basic principle of aerodynamics. Now watch.'

This time, Dr Postlethwaite kept his arms pressed against his sides, and as he lifted off, he pulled in his sizeable stomach, creating a straight line from the top of his spine to his feet. His flight was faster, smoother.

'This stuff is instinctive, though,' one of the girls muttered quietly.

Dr Postlethwaite herded the class back into the chapel. 'Homework: design and build a streamlined object, and supply a scientific explanation of your choices. Then we shall race them from the top of the dome to the cathedral floor.'

By then, it was midnight and therefore lunchtime. The croissants had helped a little, but Astrid was beginning to feel ill with hunger again. Her peripheral vision juddered slightly as they went downstairs.

The crypt canteen served up steaming bowls of spaghetti Bolognese. It was decidedly inferior to Mama's version, but Astrid still ate three portions, finally feeling a little steadier on her feet. Then the class went back upstairs to the Whispering Gallery.

Mrs Warburton taught Flight Basics, so the fledged students were taking turns flying down the nave according to her bellowed instructions. The unfledged students gathered around on the gallery to watch.

'Everyone,' Pent said. 'This is Astrid. She's new.'

The others nodded in greeting, before launching into an animated argument about whether or not they should continue to sit on the floor. Astrid could see that Mr Strangley's lesson this morning had made a lasting impression.

'It makes no sense,' Pent said. 'It's just a way of illustrating that we're not as important as the fledglings. And we already know that, so why drum it in by taking away our dignity?'

'Doesn't worry me,' said a red-haired boy with pale skin, adding to Astrid, 'I'm Tristopher te Straka, by the way. It's just sitting on the floor. They're not asking us to kneel.'

'It's the same principle though, isn't it?' Fred said. He was a quiet boy, tall and a little stooping, but when he spoke, everyone listened. 'I'll sit on the floor happily enough if there aren't enough chairs for all of us. But there are, so why should we sit on the floor as if we've done something wrong?'

'I think we should stop,' Pent said. The fledged students reappeared below, flying in an uneven V formation. Mrs Warburton was shouting about synchronising wing movement. 'We should sit on chairs.'

The others looked at her, a few of them shaking their heads.

Astrid tried to read their reaction. Was Pent well-liked? It was hard to say.

'We're lucky to be here,' said a girl with streaked hair and long earrings. 'I'm not taking any risks, even if smartie-pants over there thinks I should.'

Smartie-pants. That was directed at Pent, and hostile.

'But we're not lucky,' Tristopher said. 'It's like Mr Strangley said: we're not here by accident. We deserve to be here.'

'Easy for you to say,' the girl said.

'What's that supposed to mean?'

'You're a *te Straka*,' she snapped. 'Your family's been here for generations. I didn't even know London Overhead existed until Mrs Wairi found me a couple of months ago. None of the other externals from the real world even have their own flower, let alone a massive wealthy family dynasty of Librae to fall back on. Maybe you deserve to be here. I was lucky, and when I fledge, it will change my life, and my family's, too. I'm hoping to work as a private messenger for confidential documents, or maybe a gardener for one of the sky forests. My parents have struggled to pay rent for my entire life, and Librae jobs pay more than I'd ever dreamed. I'll sit on the floor – I'd sit anywhere if it meant I ended up with wings, and a future.'

Tristopher's cheeks turned scarlet, and he looked away.

The fledglings returned. A girl with pinkish-grey wings was flapping a little awkwardly, and Mrs Warburton was lambasting her. 'Come on now, Izzy. You've got to build your endurance. Stop giving up before you've begun!'

'Look at her go,' said a boy, raising his voice so that a girl flying past could hear him. 'Mrs Warburton doesn't take any prisoners, eh?'

'Shut up,' said the girl, swooping away.

'Mrs Warburton is Nina's mum,' Pent whispered.

'What's a te Straka?' Astrid whispered back.

'It's a surname,' Pent said. 'They're rich. The te Strakas and the Mountbattens have stacks of money. They own the Third and Fifth Flowers. Tristopher's okay, though, as te Strakas go. Marcella Mountbatten has already fledged – she's the one with the massive red kite wings – and she's less tolerable.'

'How so?' Astrid asked.

'She doesn't talk to people unless she thinks they're important. Which I guess is the long way of saying she doesn't talk to *me*. You should see her jewellery. And she has a radar bracelet.'

'What's a radar bracelet?'

Pent leant over to begin answering, but at that point, Mrs Warburton returned, and the students landed, with varying degrees of ineptitude, on the Whispering Gallery.

'All right,' Mrs Warburton barked. 'Routine flight. A short one, so don't look at me all panicked, Izzy. To the Royal Observatory in Greenwich and back. Do not land, and don't think you can avoid the full journey. I will be observing and assessing you on four criteria: stability, speed, accuracy and due caution.'

A quiet but audible groan rose from the class.

Mrs Warburton's lips thinned. 'Watch your attitude, fledglings.'

Izzy's hand was up. 'But the Observatory is beyond the Ceramicist boundaries,' she said, a whiny edge to her tone. 'What if someone sees us?'

'You can't spend forever only flying within London Overhead's borders, Izzy,' Mrs Warburton said. 'There's heavy cloud out there. Today you'll be using the flight tracking stations. We've practised this plenty of times. If you feel yourself beginning to lose control, use your flare gun.' She glanced over at the unfledged students on the benches. 'Oh, yes. You lot. Er – take notes on pages thirty-three to thirty-five in the textbook.'

Mrs Warburton turned back to the others.

'Last one back,' she said silkily, 'will be cleaning up the dead pigeons in Starminster's gutters. I believe there were six at last count.'

Immediately, there was a rush to the door. The only person who didn't hurry was the girl with auburn wings, Marcella Mountbatten, who leapt gracefully from a bench to the railing, balancing for half a second before she flew off down the nave.

'A radar bracelet,' Pent said, as though nothing had interrupted their conversation, 'tells you what else is sharing the sky. Helpful once you're out past the boundaries of the Ceramicist's enchantments. That's what Izzy was moaning about. Most of that lot will have to head straight for one of the tracking stations, at the borders of London Overhead. They'll queue up and use the tracking station to check airline flights and altitudes and calculate their speed and route. Then they'll take off with a scrappy hand drawn map and hope they don't get taken out by a 737 en route to Benidorm. Marcella doesn't have to do that, obviously. She just uses her super-pricy watch.'

'Nice,' Astrid muttered. As interesting as the whole Librae hierarchy was, it had presented a whole other issue to her mind: money.

Mama hadn't talked much about money, although *mortgage* was like a swear word. But she had drilled one fact into Astrid's head: there's no such thing as a free lunch.

Who was paying for Astrid to eat spaghetti Bolognese, or stay in the Fourth Flower? And what if she needed to buy something? She would need new clothes soon. Where would she get them?

She turned to ask Pent, but Pent was already up, backpack on. 'We've got Assembly now in the quire,' she said.

'Surely it won't start until the others get back?' Astrid said.

'True,' Pent said. 'But we need to find a seat.' She turned a brilliant, glowing smile on Astrid. 'Wouldn't want to have to sit on the floor.'

11

Astrid hurried after her, stuffing her notebook into her bag. 'But you heard what that girl said. We're lucky to be here. I don't want to get sent back to my mum.'

'You've changed your tune,' Pent retorted.

'Yeah. I know.'

Pent turned her curious gaze on Astrid. 'You going to tell me what happened?'

Astrid took a deep breath. 'Is it – is it okay if I say no?'

Pent looked at her. Astrid felt herself tense. Then she put out a hand and squeezed Astrid's tightly. 'Of course it is,' she said.

Unexpectedly, tears came to Astrid's eyes. 'Thanks.'

'That's all right. Now, back to our rebellion. We're not going to sit at the front, because that's provocative. We'll slide into the back row and save seats in case anyone wants to join us. I bet they will. Those black and white tiles look swish but they are ice-cold.'

The quire was where the choir sang: two sets of dark wooden stalls, facing one another, and intricately engraved. Again, Astrid felt a surprising wave of love. Starminster, grandeur and glory. As they slid into the benches, she looked up the organ, its pipes like gigantic knitting needles. 'I love this place,' she said quietly. 'Are you sure this is a good idea?'

'Yes. Strangley's right. It's stupid to sit on the floor. The quire is half empty at Assembly and we're all bunched up on the floor like the reception class.'

As she spoke, the rest of the class came in. Astrid watched as Fred's eyes landed on them. He said something to his companions and came over, sitting down next to them.

'All right, Fred?' Pent said.

Fred nodded. 'Hello. Welcome to Starminster, Astrid.'

'Hi,' Astrid muttered. Talking to people she didn't know was still nerve-wracking. What did they think of her? She gazed at the delicate wooden leaves embellishing her pew.

'You're right,' Fred said to Pent. 'Sitting on the floor's a joke.' He gestured towards the others. 'They'll join us – Gregory and the others.'

He was right. It took a couple of minutes of shuffling and indecision, but a few at a time, the rest of the unfledged students came over. Even the girl with the long earrings eventually sat down when she realised the alternative was sitting on the floor alone.

The fledglings began to arrive, hair standing on end or wildly tangled. Marcella Mountbatten looked smug, and Astrid knew that she had made it back first. A boy – Oscar? – was brushing pigeon feathers off his jacket, his expression cautiously blank. Older students also began to swoop down from the dome, or trickle up from lessons in the crypt or chapels.

At first, the other students more or less ignored the fifteen others in the back row. Eventually, a boy came over. 'Anton,' Pent muttered to Astrid.

'Shouldn't you be on the floor?' he said.

No one answered. Pent inflated as though she had several hundred words to say, then clamped her mouth shut.

'All of us sat on the floor until we fledged,' Anton continued. 'I don't see why you lot shouldn't. Just because some teacher says it's not on.'

'You suffered, and therefore we all should suffer,' said Rick. 'That's hardly a good reason.'

'Nothing would ever improve with that attitude,' added the

girl with the long earrings, as though she'd been supportive from the beginning.

Anton gave a tight-lipped smile. 'Right, Liane. Let's see what Finifugal has to say.'

He sat down in the front row. All at once, the little lamps went on. The organ thundered out. Astrid nearly jumped out of her skin. Around her, everyone began to sing.

And did those feet in ancient time . . .

They belted out the whole song, which sounded familiar, and Astrid watched as the teachers filed into the other side of the quire.

She saw Mr Barker, carrying an armload of messy paper. When he dropped it, another teacher knelt to help him pick it up. 'Ms Flynn. Literature of Flight,' Pent whispered. Dr Postlethwaite wore a gown like an old-fashioned schoolmaster. Mrs Warburton was flushed, Mr Strangley gave Astrid a tiny smile, and the Headmaster, who appeared last, wore a suit and a little white collar.

Astrid half-expected Mr Finifugal to climb into the pulpit, but he stood in front of the stalls, reading from a piece of paper. 'Announcements – Last departure from Starminster must be punctual, before the doors are opened to maintenance staff. Anyone leaving after 4 a.m. will be penalised. Distance flight club begins next Tuesday. First-time attendees should note the dress code. Thermal underwear is a must.' He paused to look closely at his page, and squinted up, his eyes raking over the rows.

'Where are the unfledged students?'

Pent raised her hand. One at a time, the others followed suit.

Near the back of the quire, Mr Strangley leant back and loosened his tie.

Mr Finifugal looked up at them. Astrid released a slow breath.

'Fledged students,' he said. 'Go.'

The students deployed their wings immediately and took off from within the stalls, spiralling up towards the Whispering Gallery. Astrid watched them leave, her fingernails pressing into her palms.

'Members of staff,' Mr Finifugal said, 'you are also dismissed.'

The staff flew upwards too, and Astrid had a few seconds to appreciate the difference in size between the wings of children and adults. Mr Barker's wings were white with black marks, like footprints on the snow. Mrs Warburton's were grey and pointed, her silhouette a neat arrow. Mr Strangley looked over at them. Astrid thought she read a hint of sorrow in his dark gaze. Then he opened wings as dappled as a forest floor, and swooped out of sight.

'So,' said Mr Finifugal, when Starminster was empty of Librae, 'you're too good to sit on the floor.'

No one spoke. No one moved. Mr Finifugal began to pace slowly back and forth as he spoke, his hands clasped behind his back.

'I've been considering the role of unfledged students for some time now. It strikes me as an obvious weakness in our educational system. No one benefits from the inclusion of students who can't perform the manoeuvres, who can't understand the forces we study. There are people all over the world – people in London Underfoot – people just streets away who would do anything to be in your position. And you dare to object to sitting on the floor. Your antics today demonstrate that your places here are wasted.'

The Headmaster's voice dipped into fury at the end of his sentence.

'However,' he said, 'you can certainly work. Prior to Rain Muster, London Overhead's merchants are always in need of additional help. Instead of listening to lessons on flight, which you cannot put into practice, and leaping into pews in which you have no right to sit, you will fetch and carry. Delivering packages matches your skillset, which I will remind you is minimal. Perhaps you'll think twice before beginning ludicrous rebellions with your friends.'

He paused to look at them. Astrid didn't dare meet his eyes, staring hard at one of the wooden cherubs nearby.

'Be at the Tenth Flower at 6 a.m. for your instructions.'

Pent angled her watch towards Astrid. It was already 3 a.m., and they'd been up all night.

'Starminster is off-limits to you now.' Mr Finifugal's final words were soft, barely audible. 'Get out.'

The Headmaster didn't fly. He walked, and they watched him go in silence. The quire's lights stretched out like a long thread of sunshine-coloured honey. Mr Finifugal blurred into a black scratch on Astrid's vision and disappeared.

The students broke into loud panic.

'I can't believe he's kicking us out!'

'Couriers? I'm not a courier!'

'Six in the morning?'

'I *knew* this was going to happen.'

Next to Astrid, Pent was silent. When Astrid glanced over, she saw that her eyes were full of tears. Pent kept on staring up at the ceiling, her jaw clenched, until the tears disappeared.

'This is your fault,' said Liane, pointing at Pent.

'It's not,' Fred said. 'It's the Head's fault. It's ridiculous that he's treating us like this.'

'My parents are going to kill me,' Tristopher said quietly.

A couple of others were nodding.

'We need to leave before we get into more trouble,' Liane said.

'Is he going to let us come back to Starminster when we fledge?' someone whispered.

No one answered.

* * *

They trudged back up the stairs. Astrid took one last look back at the cathedral over her shoulder. It was lit only by those small lamps, but somehow alive with glints and reflections of light.

She didn't speak as they went back up the stairs, but took comfort in the fact that Pent stayed close. The wind on the Stone Gallery was bitingly cold. Astrid wrapped her arms around herself.

'I'm going to go home,' Pent said. 'See if I can sleep for a couple hours.'

'Are your parents going to be upset?'

Pent nodded once. 'Councillor Paulson told them about my phone. They didn't really mind about that, but this . . .' She gave a shaky little laugh. 'I hate that I've disappointed them again.'

Astrid wondered if Mama was disappointed with her. But

Mama was already taking on a distant quality, only visible through glass that was becoming misty and indistinct.

'It's not your fault,' Astrid said.

Pent shrugged. 'It kind of is,' she said. 'I'll see you at six.'

Astrid took a different bridge away from Starminster. She had no intention of returning to her bubble to stew. Instead, she headed for the Tenth Flower. It was an enormous purple bloom – a verbena, perhaps – with many flowers, and the windows and balconies set into its petals glowed. She stopped in a square nearby, which featured a greenhouse full of seedlings. She found a niche under a stone wall, sheltered from the wind, and sat down.

Surely she'd fledge either way. She didn't need Starminster for that. The sky was her destiny.

But if she never learnt, if she lost the chance to be taught and guided, perhaps she'd never be able to fly freely in the sky. She'd seen how the fledglings had struggled in today's practical. She needed the help of the teachers, or her wings would be wasted. She wouldn't just lose Starminster, and its atmosphere of peace; she'd lose the sky, as well.

She imagined stepping up onto the stone wall, wings rippling out from her shoulders. How would it feel to lift away from the unrelenting suck of gravity? To belong in the sky?

She daydreamed of flight as the rising sun tinged the sky with a clearish yellow, like lemon juice. She flexed her shoulders and watched the sky turn vibrant, gaudy, drunk with colour. The first dawn she'd ever seen, and she felt the colours radiant in her eyes, in her veins, wakening parts of her that had been asleep for a long time.

Below, London Underfoot came to life. Trains slithering along their tracks, cars crawling along the streets.

When Astrid heard voices, she rose. She was cold all the way through, and half-numb. The other unfledged students were approaching from bridges all around. Astrid joined them and walked to the Tenth Flower.

The Headmaster waited in the shade of the enormous verbena, and Astrid could see that each bloom was a small apartment, joined by lifts that moved diagonally along the stems.

'Report to Fenchurch Tent. You will deliver supplies for Rain Muster. You will be working from 7 a.m. to 9 p.m. every day.'

A hand went up. 'Including weekends?'

Mr Finifugal frowned. 'Naturally, Oliver. And note you are forbidden to communicate with Starminster students. Neither will you bother members of staff. Insubordination will be disciplined.'

Astrid's one hope, appealing to Mr Strangley and hoping that he might persuade the Headmaster to change his mind, faded.

'What about our other lessons? We're going to fall behind,' Pent said.

'Education is a privilege, not a right,' Mr Finifugal said. 'You ought to know that, Penelope, with your background.'

Pent blanched.

Another hand. 'What about when we fledge?' asked Tristopher.

The Headmaster smiled. His teeth were stained and set wide apart. 'We shall have to see how your attitudes change during this time.'

Astrid felt a momentary flash of hope. Would he reconsider? Perhaps they'd get another chance.

'You will be directed further at Fenchurch Tent. Anyone suspected of malingering will be dealt with. Off you go.'

Off they went, plodding towards a navy-blue tent perched on top of the building shaped like a walkie-talkie, embroidered with gold stars and conical, like a wizard's hat. A curly-haired, freckled boy that Astrid didn't recognise was walking with Pent, his stride jaunty.

'This is Mason,' Pent said, falling into step with Astrid as though it was a foregone conclusion that she would. 'He was skiving yesterday, as usual.'

'Can you blame me?' Mason said, shaking Astrid's hand and giving her a grin. 'Another lesson with Doc Poss and I might implode. Tedium beyond belief.'

'You seem devastated to be kicked out,' Pent said drily, 'given that you so rarely attend.' She addressed Astrid. 'I can't see Mason lugging bales of clothes around for long. Doesn't like doing what he's told.'

Mason shrugged with a sunny smile. 'Too true.'

'You both seem oddly cheery,' Astrid said.

'I am cheery, actually, despite Finifugal's nasty little dig,' Pent said. 'My parents were completely supportive about the whole chair thing, would you believe? They said they were proud of me for standing up for what's right.' There was light in Pent's smile, light threaded through her hair, light in her movements, as though her joy was shining forth.

'I'd have been right there on the chairs with you if I'd known,' Mason said. 'It's pathetic how some people feel bigger by making others feel smaller. Hence my uncharacteristic attendance today.'

'Watch out – it's slippy,' Astrid said.

'Excellent observational skills,' Pent said, skipping over the green patch of lichen. 'You've only been here ten minutes and look at how streetwise you are.'

'How come bits of London Overhead are fancy, and other bits look like no one's checked on them since the Middle Ages?'

'No clue,' Pent said. 'The bathrooms are the height of luxury, though, aren't they? And I've never been inside the te Straka or Mountbatten Flowers, but I've heard rumours. They're like five-star hotels or museums or something.'

'I wonder,' Astrid said slowly, 'if the Overlords only spend money on what *they* use. You don't exactly need the bridges and staircases when you can fly, do you?'

'Maybe,' Pent said. 'The Fourth Flower's pretty nice, I suppose.'

'I heard that Mrs Wairi funded that place, though,' Mason said. 'As opposed to the Overlords.'

'Seems a shame to let old stuff get wrecked, though,' Astrid said, picking her way over broken tiles on the stairs and avoiding a gaping hole on the left. 'Why did they build it in the first place, if they were just planning to fly everywhere?'

'Maybe London Overhead was meant to be for more than just Librae,' Mason said. He speeded up a little, calling out to a girl who was walking ahead. 'Bethany! I hear you sat on a chair, you rebel!'

'Like he can stop us coming back to Starminster,' Pent said scornfully.

Astrid glanced back at the verbena. 'He is the Head.'

'Please. According to my dad, he's mostly the Head because he works in Starminster during the day. He's a chaplain or something.'

'Imagine you need some help with your prayers or whatever and Mr Terrifying Finifugal comes parading in. I can literally imagine nothing worse,' Astrid said with a shudder.

Pent laughed, long and loud, and Astrid felt a strange leap of pride.

'There's something about you, Astrid,' she said.

Astrid paused. Friendship still felt like a marshy landscape, riddled with sinkholes and sharp rocks. But she wanted to say something, even if it was strange, to show Pent that she was grateful.

'Thank you for being so nice to me,' Astrid said. 'You've – you've made me feel like you want me around. And I've got sort of a weird background.'

'We've all got weird backgrounds,' Pent said bluntly. 'But I like you, too. I'm glad you decided to stay.'

12

The man in charge of Fenchurch Tent introduced himself as Merchant Abebe, and handed out the assignments swiftly. 'Rain Muster is coming upon us quickly, and art supplies need to be transported from the delivery points in the city below so that the artists can purchase them from my shop,' he said. 'Your help will contribute to a glorious exhibition this year. Many of the supplies are fragile, so I urge you to handle them with care.' He paused. 'I realise this is a disciplinary situation, but I want to emphasise that you must not overload yourselves. You could do permanent damage to your backs and shoulders, and that'll do you no favours once you fledge.'

He paired Astrid with Tristopher te Straka, and Pent with Rick Prankel. Mason was paired with Fred Moutts.

'The usual rules,' Merchant Abebe said. 'Act with due caution. Do not court attention from Underfooters or talk to strangers. If you think you are being watched, don't use the transition points until you are unobserved.'

He handed Astrid and Tristopher a sheet of paper with an address and a map on it. 'You will be transporting clay.'

Pent and Rick were assigned to oil paints. The others were allocated to a range of items to pick up from collection points all over the city: charcoals, ink bottles, glue, canvas, tools, fabric.

'Use the lift on the Fifth Flower. The Mountbattens have graciously granted permission,' Merchant Abebe said. 'I'll expect everyone back within the hour.'

They walked to the Fifth Flower, a crimson dahlia, and compared notes while waiting for the lift.

'We've got to pick ours up from an Amazon locker,' said Rick.

'Ours is a random address,' Tristopher said. 'Clay's heavy, isn't it? What an absolute fiasco.'

'Worried about your poor little back?' said Liane, who seemed to have an especial venom reserved for Tristopher.

'Obviously,' Tristopher muttered. 'Can't buy a new spine.'

'I can agree with that,' Liane said.

The lift arrived and they crowded in.

The lift doors opened directly into a busy street. They traipsed out into the crowd.

When Astrid looked back, the doors of the lift slid into invisibility behind plywood panels. A sign on them declared 'Apologies for our appearance'. Astrid nudged Tristopher and said, 'How do we get back?'

'Relax,' Tristopher said. 'You press the first "o" of "apologies". It's a hidden button.'

He consulted the map. 'This way, then right,' he said, and strutted off into the crowd.

Astrid followed, hunching her shoulders over. She glanced up. It was comforting to see the bridges and staircases weaving overhead, but the Librae who flew were distant as birds in the sky. She felt very small.

'Don't stare up like that,' Tristopher said as they walked down the street. 'The Underfooters can't see London Overhead, remember?'

'Maybe I'm looking at that skyscraper,' Astrid said.

'The Walkie-Talkie, it's nicknamed,' Tristopher said. 'Apparently, it melted a car one time. The architects didn't realise that the windows would focus a beam of light directly onto the street.'

'Ouch,' Astrid muttered.

'It was a Jag,' said Tristopher mournfully. 'I'm sure the owner was devastated.'

It was so crowded that walking was like a sport, dodging and weaving between frowning people. Astrid found herself wishing for the peaceful solitude of London Overhead, despite its crumbling architecture.

Tristopher stopped. 'This is the place,' he said, opening the door and going inside. It was a quiet shop, and when they asked about the clay, the shopkeeper showed them downstairs into a basement, saying doubtfully, 'You two seem a little young to be working as couriers.'

'We're on work experience,' Tristopher said glibly.

The shopkeeper shook his head. 'Watch your backs, then, kids. It's exploitative, that's what it is.'

'Agreed,' Astrid murmured.

The basement floor was covered in sacks.

'All for us, presumably,' Tristopher said with a groan.

Astrid opened one of the sacks and peered inside the plastic wrapping.

'It's silver,' she said, delighted. 'Look – it sparkles. It must be mixed with silver particles.'

'Bet it weighs a ton,' said Tristopher. 'Didn't Barker say something about silver and Rain Muster?'

'People believed it purified the rainwater.'

'If I had a silver car,' said Tristopher, heaving a sack into his arms, 'I'd go with white leather for the seats.'

Astrid hefted one of the sacks over her shoulder. It was unbelievably heavy.

'But if my car was red, which I think I'd prefer,' Tristopher continued as they marched up the stairs and back onto the street, 'I think black would be more striking.'

This was Astrid's introduction to Tristopher's obsession, which she heard about more or less continually throughout the day as they lugged bags of silver clay up to Fenchurch Tent. It made sense, she reflected. If Tristopher was incredibly rich, he'd no doubt been given everything he wanted from day one. But you couldn't have a car in London Overhead.

At night, Astrid returned to the Fourth Flower. She ate a sandwich from a seemingly bottomless refrigerator, wished she had the time and energy to swim in the pool, and tried to sleep. Every night, her sleep was tainted by nightmares where she dreamt of falling into the labyrinthine, chaotic streets of London Underfoot.

She didn't see much of Pent, except for the day when the oil paint leaked and Pent's hands were rainbow-streaked.

'Does this stain?' Pent shouted, and Astrid laughed until

Pent ran up to her and pressed her hands against Astrid's cheeks, smearing colour all over her.

* * *

On their fifth day in London Underfoot, Astrid saw a television screen in the window of a shop, and recognised her own face.

ASTRID CROSSLEY: MISSING FOR A FULL WEEK.

In smaller letters, it said, *RUNAWAY?*

Tristopher glanced at the screen, but before he could process what he'd seen, Astrid said, 'Hey, is that a Ferrari?'

Tristopher's head twisted so speedily that she thought it might fall off. 'For goodness' sake, Astrid,' he said irritably. 'It's a Porsche. They aren't even close to the same. Look at the silhouette, to begin with.'

'It's the horse emblems on them both. Confusing,' Astrid said. She had learned more about Ferraris in the last five days than she had ever wanted to know.

'It's linked to their origin, actually. They're both made in the same part of Germany,' Tristopher said, and Astrid looked back as they walked on. The picture was still on the screen, and in front of it, a female reporter was talking rapidly with a furrowed brow. The picture flashed to a stage, where Mama stood in front of a microphone.

Her heart sank. The note to Mama had done nothing to reassure her, then. It still seemed like a terrible risk to report that Astrid had gone. Surely questions would be asked of Mama about the mysterious daughter that no one had ever met.

But how many times had Mama told Astrid that she would do anything for her? Astrid should have known that Mama would leave no stone unturned to find her daughter.

It occurred to Astrid that she needed to hide her hair. It was long and light, and though far from unique, it might be unusual enough to catch someone's eye.

She borrowed a hat from Pent that evening, and wore it for the next few days. With her hair tucked away inside it, no one looked at her twice. She saw more 'missing' posters, stuck to lampposts, on the sides of the red buses. Images of her face, multiplying every day.

Six tedious, exhausting days later, Astrid and Tristopher finished carrying the silver clay and were reassigned to chips of gold for the sculptors. Liane and her work partner Clair were openly envious. Their job had robbed them of their sense of humour – they were carrying boxes of stained glass, fragile and heavy.

'Want to swap?' Clair had shouted over the wind. 'Give me something that doesn't smash if I drop it!'

'At least you're not a target for every thief in London Underfoot,' Tristopher had shouted back. Astrid assumed he was joking, until Tristopher continued to fret.

'I swear, if I get mugged over this, my parents will be straight to the Overlords to report that Finifugal's putting us in *mortal danger*. The man should be sacked,' he said. 'They're already outraged that I'm missing out on educational opportunities.'

'I bet they are,' said Astrid. She was developing a liking for Tristopher, with his air of pomposity. There was something unashamedly vulgar about it. Pent called him Tacky Tristopher behind his back. 'I quite like the gold, though. Makes me feel fancy.' She shook the parcel she carried, and it tinkled gently.

The lift doors opened on London Overhead. It was getting dark, but the city below sparkled.

They delivered the gold parcels to Merchant Abebe, who weighed them carefully. Pent arrived at the same time, taking off her backpack. This time, her T-shirt was stained all down the back with chartreuse paint.

'Before you start, it is not my fault that the delivery people in London Underfoot don't put the lids on the paint tubes properly,' she said to Merchant Abebe.

'It is, however, your fault that you don't *check* beforehand,' Merchant Abebe said.

'Last job of the day, boss. Skip the lecture. Mum is making nihari.'

'Rain Muster begins in less than two weeks,' Merchant Abebe said. 'Maybe sooner, if the forecast is right.'

'But nihari is tonight,' Pent said with a wide grin. 'See you tomorrow. I'll be sure to screw all the lids on extra tight.'

Merchant Abebe turned away, unable to hide his smile.

Tristopher sauntered off to the luxury of the Fifth Flower, and Pent and Astrid set out together.

'Did you hear the news?' Pent said.

'No?'

'Fred Moutts fledged.'

'When?'

'Last night. He was in his nesthome with his family. I think it only took a few hours for his wings to come in. A couple of other people were feeling a bit off too, so there might be more soon.'

'A few *hours*?'

'Obviously,' said Pent. 'It's not the same as people deploying their wings, which you've seen loads of times. The wings have to break through the skin. I hear it twinges a bit.'

'Whoa. You never mentioned this!'

'Sorry, sorry. I forget how embarrassingly ignorant you are.'

'Charming.'

'It's magical as well, of course,' Pent said. 'It changes everything.'

Astrid found her hands reaching over her shoulder and running along her smooth skin, imagining the skin parting to make way for wings. She hoped they'd be beautiful. But she also knew that she wouldn't really care, as long as they launched her into the sky. She imagined stepping off the bridge, and her wings opening up to catch her, and felt a swoop of excitement.

'I'll see you soon,' Astrid said, as they came to the turning towards the Fourth Flower.

'Where are you going?' Pent demanded.

'Back to the Fourth Flower? Like always?'

'I said we were having nihari! I couldn't go home and eat nihari knowing that you were stuck having sandwiches yet again.'

'Oh,' Astrid said, warmth igniting inside her. 'Thanks for inviting me. I'd love to have nihari with you.'

'I have to warn you,' Pent said, 'the house is teeny. And we sit on the floor to eat.'

'That's – that will be lovely,' Astrid said eagerly.

They walked together to Pent's nesthome. It hung like a limpet from the Eleventh Flower, a daffodil, one of hundreds, and impossible to distinguish from the others. 'How do you know which one's yours?' Astrid said, and Pent replied, 'I follow my nose, to be honest.'

She wasn't wrong. A savoury aroma soon wafted by, and Astrid could smell cardamom and cumin.

Pent's mother, Mrs Hayat, was waiting near the entrance. She swept Pent into an embrace, saying, 'I always worry about you! What's this paint, my love? Why can't you check the lids are on tight?'

'I'm so desperately hungry by the end of the day that I can't worry about little things like lids,' Pent said from the midst of her mother's crushing embrace. Her cheeks were squashed, and she rolled her eyes, grinning. 'If you'll let go, I can introduce Astrid.'

Mrs Hayat released Pent and said, 'I have heard so much about you, Astrid. Apparently you've been surviving on a diet of sandwiches!'

Astrid smiled a little awkwardly. 'Thank you for having me,' she said.

Mrs Hayat was elegant and wore a lot of jewellery. Astrid pushed aside a flap of canvas, then a jangling bead curtain. The nesthome's interior, as Pent had warned her, was cramped. Coloured cloth hung from the walls, and on a hotplate, the nihari simmered. 'This is Dad and this is Polly,' Pent said, pointing to a man and a little girl.

Before Astrid could look around properly, she was sitting on the floor with a bowl of nihari. Lemon slices, green chillies and naan bread were pressed upon her. She accepted them all and began to eat. The nihari was delectable, steaming and spicy.

Mrs Hayat watched her with satisfaction. 'You've been eating too little, my dear,' she said.

'I'm still getting used to life here, I suppose,' Astrid said.

'The food in the Fourth Flower is so bland,' Mr Hayat said. 'We do struggle to cook in this small space. No stove, you see.'

'We make do with a hot plate. And there's a communal oven out on the Eleventh Flower where Aadil bakes naan,' Mrs Hayat explained. 'Not that either of us have much time to cook. Work is busy.'

'Do you work up here?' Astrid asked.

'In a manner of speaking,' Mrs Hayat said. 'I'm a financial consultant working from home. Little do my non-Librae colleagues know that I'm only a few metres above them in the digital library on the Seventh Flower! Aadil works for the Overlords, however. He's a landscape architect.'

'I didn't know there was a digital library,' Astrid said.

'Oh, yes. Because the nesthomes are so tiny, many Librae

work there. Careers exclusive to Librae become riskier every year. The mortality rate is concerning, so I try to encourage Pent to work hard, so that she can be employed in London Underfoot.'

'Why – why do you live here, if you work down there?' Astrid asked.

Mrs Hayat gave a melancholy smile, the creases on her forehead deepening. 'It's safe to fly freely here.'

Mr Hayat handed Astrid another piece of naan.

'I've got a new project,' he said to his wife, 'sorting out that sky forest over Manchester. Dutch elm disease is doing some terrible damage. We're trying to stop the spread, but the forest has been decimated.'

Pent turned to Astrid to explain, 'Dad's in charge of landscaping the sky forests. He's an expert in ecosystems, so he designed the one over Canary Wharf. Apparently it's halved the carbon dioxide levels in that area.'

'I'd love to explore it properly,' Astrid said.

'Maybe we could sneak over there, some day after work.'

'Mum and Dad would kill you,' said Polly smugly.

'Shut up, Apolla.'

'Don't call me that!'

'It's your name, isn't it?' Pent turned back to Astrid. 'Mum and Dad love mythology, hence Penelope and Apolla.'

'Apolla's a stupid name,' Polly muttered.

'Apolla,' Mr Hayat said warningly. 'No need to be rude.'

'Pent's planning to break more rules!'

'You're always trying to get me into trouble,' Pent hissed.

'Not my fault you make it so easy,' her sister said, grinning.

Astrid, sitting in the centre of this bickering, warm, loving family, felt a film of unreality settle over her. Their conversation seemed to hush. How she had longed for this warmth, this home. A family eating a meal together.

And Mama had tried. She'd brought dinner and they had sat together. Sometimes they'd played cards, or watched something. But nothing could change the fact that Mama had new stories to tell every day, and Astrid did not. Unexpectedly, she felt a surge of anger. Mama had kept her in the shed all this time, because she didn't want Astrid to have wings. As if wings were something awful! And she'd deprived her of this, as well. Of the ease and comfort of a family, and a home.

It was wonderful to sit here and eat with Pent's family. And yet it was painful, because even if Astrid fledged, and even if she was allowed back into Starminster, she would never have a family like this. Bickering and laughing and loving one another, as if it were part of an ordinary day. As if it were nothing.

13

After dinner they ate hot, sweet jalebis for dessert, and Astrid took her leave. She felt a pang as Pent waved goodbye at the door and returned to the warmth of her home. She walked back to the Fourth Flower slowly, pausing to note down hazards on her route as always, then took a new staircase that led down towards the river.

She stopped above the Thames. The stairs dropped low enough that she could hear the hum of conversation rising from the Millennium Bridge. Lights shimmered in the water; ice-blue, golden, a faint pink.

Above, London Overhead was a black scrawl on the sky. The First Flower, a tropical, crimson thing, glowed overhead. Who lived in it?

If only she could ask Mr Barker. For weeks, questions had been mounting up within her. In the river, the reflection of Starminster shone like a pearl.

A spine-chilling shriek.

For a second, she thought it was human, but when it was joined by a chorus of others, she realised that it was a bird.

Astrid followed the noise and found the birds in a square bordered with olive trees. They had gathered to eat some scattered seeds, and now their feet were stuck in whatever had been smeared on the ground. Tar, maybe?

Ten starlings, their yellow beaks open in appeal.

Mr Finifugal stood above them.

A gasp escaped Astrid's mouth.

'Astrid Crossley,' said Mr Finifugal. 'What are you doing here?'

Astrid's hands were shaking.

'What are you doing?' she said. Her voice was high-pitched. 'Please don't hurt them.'

Mr Finifugal shrugged. 'It's science, I'm afraid. The pursuit of knowledge leaves no room for tender feelings.'

She shook her head, hand to her mouth, unable to speak.

'You might have noticed, in your brief time here, that we have plenty of physicists, any number of botanists, a historian here, a philosopher there, but no biologists. We are an ancient people, yet our predecessors lacked the stomach and the ambition to know more about the true nature of Libraekind, and as a result we are profoundly uneducated about ourselves.'

'Does it matter?' Astrid said hoarsely.

'Of course it does. The Overlords don't support my research; they want to retain the mystique, the magic of Libraekind. But ignorance doesn't serve anyone. We don't even know where our wings go when they aren't in use. Older Librae struggle with wing atrophy and delayed wing deployment, but we haven't got a hope of solving these issues while we know so little.'

'These birds aren't Librae, though,' Astrid said, gesturing at the starlings. They fluttered their wings in response.

'No. But they are creatures of flight, and we have much to learn from them. Can we improve our flight time through strengthening certain muscles, or through diet? Can we gain an instinctive sense of direction? All of this can be learned from studying the birds.'

Astrid paused. 'I wish – I wish you wouldn't,' she said.

Mr Finifugal's laugh became a snarl. 'Go home, girl. I've got dozens of experiments under way. We must all make sacrifices in the name of science.'

Defeated, Astrid gave the birds one more hopeless look, turned, and walked away.

The Fourth Flower's pool was empty of children, the waterfall slowed to a drip. Astrid went down to the edge to dip her feet in the cool water. It was soothing on her blistered heels.

She hadn't noticed the lack of biology on the curriculum in the little time she'd had at Starminster, but now that Mr Finifugal had raised it, she saw it was true. She, too, had a scientific mind; she understood Mr Finifugal's curiosity about the Librae body, and understood, also, the value of knowing how it worked.

But . . . it disturbed her. Those helpless birds.

*   *   *

The next day, she felt sluggish and weary when she crawled out of bed. It was a Monday, and the city below was swarming with tourists, even at this early hour. She watched their movement from above, gratified by her growing ability to walk the bridges with confidence, avoiding weakened planks and potholes, piecing together the occasional shortcut.

When she arrived at Fenchurch Tent, Tristopher was waiting, staring down longingly at a gleaming car below.

'You're picking up beads today,' said Merchant Abebe.

Astrid and Tristopher were on their way to the lift when they passed Mason, the boy Pent had introduced her to a few days earlier. He was sitting on a bench with a view into the Walkie-Talkie's Sky Garden.

'Hello,' he said. His hair stood out in a wiry shock, and his gap-toothed smile was wide and welcoming.

'Shouldn't you be, er . . .' Tristopher said.

'I've had quite enough of courier work,' Mason said breezily. 'Dull and surprisingly strenuous. And Fred cleared off to fledge, so I'm hardly taking up the burden by myself. I'm just deciding what to eat for breakfast.' He pointed at a pair of men on the other side of the glass digging into their breakfast. 'I like the look of the raspberry and white chocolate muffin, but I'm also tempted by the smoked salmon and cream cheese bagel.'

'It's hardly cheap in there,' Tristopher said, with the air of a connoisseur.

'I won't be paying,' Mason said. 'There's a hatch at the back for ventilation. Swing it open, climb in and you can help yourself to the food right before it goes out. I've never been spotted, and I'm sneaky enough that I never will.'

'Bit dishonest,' Tristopher said, frowning.

'Where did you say the hatch was?' Astrid said.

'Ah, there you have it,' Mason said, leading Astrid over to

an inconspicuous grille and showing her how to swing it open. 'Astrid, like me, has had enough Fourth Flower cheese sandwiches to last her the rest of her life. Not all of us are dining Michelin-style every night, te Straka.'

Astrid felt oddly defensive of Tristopher, who looked mortified, maybe even a little teary. 'Tristopher's been working really hard,' she said.

'Nothing like teamwork,' Mason said. His voice was so upbeat and sprightly that she almost missed the sarcasm. 'Would you like me to grab you something to eat?' he went on, adding with a shrug, 'No one suffers. They assume they misread the order, and make another, and all is well.'

Astrid glanced at Tristopher sidelong, expecting disapproval. To her surprise, he grinned. 'Why not, when you put it like that?' he said. 'I'll take a muffin.'

'Same,' Astrid said.

Mason clambered into the hatch on the side of the skyscraper and Astrid and Tristopher took his place on the bench, watching the people. It was rather disconcerting, everyone staring right at the spot they were sitting and pointing out of the enormous window, even though Astrid knew it was the view they were looking at, and not them.

'I feel like I'm on stage,' Tristopher said uneasily.

'Imagine if they could see us.'

'Mass hysteria, I expect.' Tristopher reached out and pulled a lever next to him, and the bench rotated gently to face the sunrise. 'Not bad, is it, London Overhead?'

'Your family must have lived here for a while,' Astrid said.

'Oh, certainly. Aeons, I should think,' he said airily. 'My father's a bit of a history buff. Always on the hunt for ancestors to add to the family tree.'

'D'you think he ever met . . .' Astrid hesitated. 'Could you ask him about someone called Erika Crossley?'

'A relative?' Tristopher asked.

'Mm,' Astrid said.

'Librae?'

'No. Well, I don't think so.'

'If she's a Librae, she'll have scars on her back. All fledged Librae have them when their wings are tucked away.'

Astrid hadn't thought of that. Since finding the initials scratched on the wood up at Crow's Nest, she'd felt more and more sure that Mama *was* a Librae, and that she'd lied about her birthday for some mysterious reason. Astrid had imagined her with pale-grey dove wings. But there was no denying that Mama's back was smooth and unmarked.

'If she isn't a Librae, Dad won't know her,' Tristopher said

136

confidently. 'He's barely met an unfledged person in his life. Hasn't set foot out of the Third Flower in years.'

'What's the Third Flower like?'

'I ought to be upper-crust and downplay it, really,' Tristopher said. 'But it's been a thoroughly top-notch place to grow up. Pleasant rooms. Gorgeous gardens. There're even wind tunnels down in the stem cellars where you can practise flying. Highly recommend it.'

'What, wealth?'

'Well, yes, frankly.'

Mason came out with a brown paper bag and dispensed white chocolate and raspberry muffins, still warm from the oven. Astrid devoured hers blissfully.

'Thank you,' Tristopher said, nibbling a piece.

'Yes, thanks,' Astrid echoed.

'My pleasure,' Mason said, suddenly courtly.

'Aren't you worried Finifugal will come looking for you, and you'll get into trouble?' Astrid asked.

Mason waved a hand. 'I've got my doubts. In my experience, teachers haven't got the time or inclination to carry out half their threats. Finifugal talks big, and the merchant chap seems reasonably decent, but if you ask me, they just fancied a bit of free labour.'

'I don't know,' Tristopher said. 'Finifugal certainly looked shocked when he saw us sitting on the chairs.'

Mason's laughter was bitter as espresso. 'Unbelievable. Sitting on chairs, an act of rebellion. I thought I'd left all that rubbish behind when I came here. I suppose bureaucracy's everywhere.'

'What kind of rubbish did you leave behind?'

'My parents are poor,' Mason said bluntly. 'School was tough. Everything was tough. They didn't really get me, couldn't exactly afford me, so I . . . well, I jumped at the chance when Mrs Wairi offered it to me. Jumped with both feet.'

Astrid looked from Mason to Tristopher. One living a life of luxury, casually recommending wealth; the other with a family who couldn't afford him. But they were both here, both hoping for wings, and – until Mr Finifugal's ridiculous edict – learning from the same teachers. It made her feel hopeful.

She patted Mason on the shoulder. 'We'd better be off. Thanks again.'

'No bother,' Mason said.

As they trooped off to the Fifth Flower, Astrid glanced back. Mason was lying on the bench, feet up, his hands under his head as if relaxing at the seaside. She felt a flicker of envy for his lack of concern, his certainty that he belonged in London Overhead.

In the lift, Astrid pulled her hat over her hair. Tristopher was analysing the pros and cons of Japanese cars as opposed to German ones.

'Any word about Fred? Is he back in Starminster now?' Astrid asked when he paused for breath.

'I heard his mum and dad have taken him to the Fourth Flower to meet with Finifugal,' Tristopher said with a grimace. 'Hope they crack the whip a bit. He can't keep us out of education once we've fledged.'

'What do you think of him?' Astrid asked, keeping her voice light. She thought of the birds, trapped and crying out in fear.

'My parents reckon he's more interested in science than education. He mostly got the Headmaster job because he's a chaplain. Useful to have a Librae with an Underfoot role in the cathedral. He knows the timetables, codes for the alarms, has all the keys. His wife's not Librae, I heard.'

'He's into biology, right?'

The lift opened and they turned out into the street.

'Yep. Had a theory for a while that you could grow Librae wings from a single feather. Nonsense, if you ask me. He's forever begging my family for funds. I'm fairly certain Dad paid for his laboratory on the Fourth Flower just to make him go away.'

Astrid laughed. Then her gaze caught on something.

A woman stood in a doorway talking on the phone, her fair hair tousled in the petrol-scented breeze. For a second, Astrid thought she was Mama – for a second, she looked into the woman's eyes.

But a second was long enough. Recognition dawned, the woman's face lighting up.

'It's the missing girl!' the woman said, and Astrid, idiot that she was, flinched.

The woman's hand shot out and she caught hold of Astrid's arm, her voice rising in pitch as she shouted to the people around her. 'It's her! It's Astrid Crossley, the missing child!'

14

Tristopher reached for Astrid, alarm in his eyes, but a crowd was already gathering.

'Call the police!' the woman bellowed. 'Call 999!'

Someone else snatched the hat off Astrid's head.

'It's definitely her,' a girl said intently. 'I recognise those eyes.'

'Tristopher!' Astrid gasped. 'Run!'

She wasn't sure that he would hear her – he had disappeared into the crowd, and the woman's arm was around her. She was saying, 'Now, now, love, you're safe. We'll get you back to your mum.'

'No, wait,' Astrid said, too late. Phones were pointing at her. Astrid tried to shield her face, certain she was being filmed.

'Looks like she had just run away from home. Thank goodness she's all right,' someone said.

'You are okay, right?' the woman said. 'The police are on their way. Should I ask for an ambulance too?'

'No,' Astrid said. 'I'm not Astrid, I'm not!'

'It's her! Look at the mole next to her ear!'

Flashing blue lights. Astrid caught a glimpse of Tristopher's face in the crowd, his stricken expression.

Two police officers broke through the crush, their arms outstretched. 'Give her space, everyone, give her space.'

A policewoman gripped Astrid's shoulders.

'I'm not Astrid!'

'We're going to take you to the police station. Don't be scared.'

'But I'm not Astrid!'

'Come along, dear . . .' The policewoman pushed her gently towards a police car, into the back seat and shut the door.

Astrid pulled on the handle, but it was locked, and there was a fine mesh between her and the front seat. Astrid's shock was dispersing, making way for horrified alarm. What would happen? They would send for Mama. To come and get her.

And Astrid knew, more fiercely than ever before, that she would fight every step of the way. She would never go back into that rhubarb shed again.

The opposite door opened, and the policewoman climbed in. She had a blanket in her arms, which she offered to Astrid.

'You must be cold,' she said. 'My name's Pauline, Astrid. I'm going to make sure that you get home safely.'

'I'm not Astrid,' Astrid said, and she wasn't cold, either; sweat was gathering, slick on her spine, on her face. 'I'm Sarah, I'm on my way to school! Let me out!'

'Okay, okay,' Pauline said, and Astrid thought that she might believe her. Instead, she said gently, 'And where do you go to school, Sarah?'

She was just humouring her. Astrid let out a strangled sound of anger and frustration as she yanked at the door handle again. Outside the window, dozens of people had gathered, and many were filming, their phones lights dazzling.

'You were home-schooled, isn't that right?' Pauline said gently. 'Your mother says you're advanced for your age. Not many friends. A bit isolated. Scared of going outside.'

Astrid stopped pulling at the door. So that was Mama's explanation for her daughter's invisible existence. A hysterical giggle rose to her lips, and she fought it back down.

'Are you hungry, Astrid?'

'I'm not Astrid.'

'Here, take the blanket. You should be wearing a coat – I know it's only September, but it's already getting chilly.'

Would anyone from London Overhead come to get her? Tristopher would raise the alarm, surely. But Mr Finifugal would be more than happy to hear she'd gone. Pent would be upset. Mrs Wairi, she thought, would be disappointed that after the ordeal of taking Astrid to London Overhead, she hadn't stuck it out. But a couple of weeks ago, Astrid had been telling anyone who would listen that she was going home as soon as possible. Everyone might assume that Astrid had done a runner.

The other officer got into the driving seat.

Pauline tapped the screen of her phone, then held it up and spoke softly. Astrid listened.

'It's definitely her. Yes, she's here with me now.' She listened, then said, 'Sure, put the mother through.' Another pause. 'Hello, Erika. Yes, Astrid's right here. Of course you can.'

She said gently to Astrid, 'It's your mum, Astrid. She wants a word.'

She handed Astrid the phone. The glass rectangle was unwieldy and slippery in her hands. Astrid lifted it up to her ear, arms heavy as lead.

'Astrid, hello. Astrid, it's Mama.'

Her voice. Exactly the same. As if Mama were sitting next to her.

Astrid's grip on the phone tightened. A part of her longed to reach into the phone and pull Mama into her arms. To feel Mama stroke her hair, to be held like she was a little child. She could almost smell her – vanilla and rosemary, raspberry jam and fresh scones.

But she didn't want to leave London Overhead. Not yet – not when she had just made friends, her future as a Librae beckoning.

'Listen to me, Astrid. I'm on my way, darling. Don't go anywhere, you hear me? Just wait – I'm coming. Astrid, things will be different now. I promise. We'll see if we can get you started at school, all right? I've got your bedroom all ready for you, right next to mine, in the farmhouse. Like you always wanted.'

Astrid didn't speak. It felt as though a shard of crystal had grown in her throat.

'Say something, darling. Just tell me you're all right.'

Mama's voice, full of warmth and love. She wouldn't say it on the phone – she couldn't, without risking suspicion from the police – but Astrid was certain that Mama knew where she'd been. She knew about London Overhead.

'Okay, I understand. You don't want to talk. But Astrid, you must listen to me. Please don't go anywhere. Don't run away from the police. They'll keep you safe, yes? You can trust them. Darling, I'll be there soon.'

Pauline held out her hand, and Astrid returned the phone. She spoke into it. 'She's not saying much, I'm afraid. Yes, physically she seems fine. Right, then we'll see you in a few hours. Of course. You're not to worry. Astrid will be with you soon. Bye, then.' She tapped the screen again, then said to Astrid, 'We're going to the hospital to get you checked out.'

Panic was beginning to wrap itself around Astrid's neck. Mama was on her way, and she would never let Astrid return to London Overhead, whether she fledged or not – Mama would never risk losing her again.

Was she telling the truth about the farmhouse; about going to school? She remembered what she'd overheard Mrs Wairi saying to Mr Finifugal. *Further reinforcements to the shed.*

And even if Mama was telling the truth, it wasn't enough any more. Astrid needed to be in London Overhead, she needed to learn how to fly in Starminster. She was a Librae, now. She wasn't going to give that up.

Maybe if she fledged right now? She reached over her shoulders to feel her back, hoping that a feather might poke through. But even then, she would be trapped here. And no one from London Overhead could rescue her from a police car.

Pauline was tapping away on her phone. Then she said gently, 'Astrid, I don't want to hassle you too much with questions, not until your mum arrives. But there's one thing I need to check immediately. Is that all right?'

'I'm not Ast—'

Pauline interrupted. 'This question is urgent. It can't wait. Wherever you've been the last few days, have there been other children?'

A turquoise vein was standing out in Pauline's temple, and she was staring at Astrid, her shoulders tense.

Astrid didn't reply. Of course there had been other children. The other Starminster students. Pent, Tristopher, Mason, Fred, Liane. Loads of children.

'The thing is,' Pauline said after a long silence, 'a number of children have recently gone missing in London. Their disappearance wasn't initially linked to your case, which of course happened all the way in Yorkshire, but now that we've found you in London, we have to ask.'

Astrid looked down at her knees, saying nothing. As far as she knew, Mrs Wairi and the other acquirers had not brought any other children to London Overhead since her, or in the weeks leading up to her arrival; she had been the newest student at Starminster. Those missing children couldn't have anything to do with the Librae.

Pauline gave a barely audible sigh.

'The children who disappeared were about your age, but they came from difficult backgrounds,' she went on. 'As a result, it took us some time to link their disappearances to one another. Some of the parents were unreliable. Others aren't sure when they last saw their children. Astrid, it's important that you tell the truth. Have you seen any of these children?'

Pauline tapped on her phone again and showed Astrid a picture of a boy, then flicked through several photographs. Girls and boys. None were familiar.

Astrid shook her head.

'We have one witness,' Pauline said. 'A thirteen-year-old who was asleep in his mother's room at a women's shelter. He woke as his little sister was being taken, just two days ago. His description was minimal – it was dark, and he only noticed that the man was Caucasian, and older. He also said that the man had . . . well, wings. Like a bird. Feathers down his back.'

Astrid's head snapped up.

'You've reacted to that, Astrid,' Pauline said.

Astrid looked at her warily.

'Does that description mean something to you?'

Of course it did. It meant that a Librae had been stealing children. And not acquiring them like Mrs Wairi, bringing them straight to Starminster to begin their Librae education, but – doing something else with them. What?

'No,' Astrid said, but inside her head, everything was swirling.

The boy had seen a man with wings. Whoever had taken the sister must have thought that everyone was asleep, and hadn't hidden their wings as carefully as they should.

'The wings thing, Astrid. Does it sound . . . in any way . . . similar to someone you've met recently?'

'No,' Astrid said.

'We thought perhaps a cape, or a big coat.'

'I don't know anything about that.'

'All right, then,' Pauline said.

'What kind of bird, though?' Astrid said. She tried to keep her tone casual, but by the lift of Pauline's eyebrows, she had failed.

'I don't believe the boy mentioned that.'

'How many children are gone?' Astrid asked. She knew she should keep quiet, but she had to know.

Again, Pauline's face twitched. 'Five,' she said. 'Five in the past five weeks. We hope they'll be found soon. Like you were.

149

Now, we're off to St Thomas' Hospital. They'll check you out for shock, dehydration, etcetera.'

'I don't want . . .' Astrid said.

Then the spark of an idea began to glimmer, red-hot, in her mind. St Thomas' Hospital. She'd heard that name somewhere recently.

'Actually, yes. I feel a bit dizzy.'

'Goodness, you change your mind quickly,' Pauline remarked.

'I'm very traumatised,' Astrid said.

For a second, she thought Pauline might laugh. Instead, she reapplied her sympathetic frown, and said, 'Of course.'

The name. Where had she heard it?

Of course. Mrs Wairi had pointed it out. The emergency red slide in the Fourth Flower, which led directly to St Thomas' Hospital's A&E.

That was a stroke of luck.

The car was slowing.

'Are we nearly there?' Astrid said.

Pauline nodded.

Astrid looked out of the window. There was a clear run of about twenty feet between the hospital doors and the police car. She spotted the red slide, which snaked down out of the sky and ended right by the hospital entrance.

Astrid took several deep breaths as she waited for Pauline to open her door. As she got out, she glanced up at the sky.

London Overhead, the flowers wide, drinking in the sunlight. Stairs and bridges, weaving over and under one another. Splendid, ancient, bewildering, spiderweb city. A single word rang out like a bell in her mind: *Home. Home. Home.*

She ran.

She dashed towards the hospital entrance, feet and arms flying, air pumping in and out of her, running – running as fast as she could towards the hospital entrance. Pauline was after her instantly, shouting, *'Astrid!'*

Astrid glanced over her shoulder and saw Pauline slow a little, her expression bewildered, when she realised that Astrid was heading directly for the hospital entrance. But at the last second, Astrid veered right and flung herself into the mouth of the slide.

She lay still for a second, catching her breath. Pauline's footsteps were getting closer, and then she could see her, gazing around wildly, mystified.

She could hear her own breathing, magnified in the metal tube, and the clang of her movements.

It had worked. The Ceramicists' enchantment had held firm. Astrid's heart pounded as Pauline walked over to the slide and straight through it, like a ghost. She was invisible. Insubstantial.

She remembered Pent's words about airplanes passing through the city, through Pent's own body. It made her feel strange. But she was safe now.

Pauline was shouting into her radio, 'Set up a perimeter! *Now!*' She was calling Astrid's name, her voice panicked.

Astrid felt a brief flash of guilt. A posse of police officers ran past the slide, chatter on their radios loud and full of static.

She took off her shoes and socks, briefly noted how sweaty and sticky her hands and feet were, and began to climb.

It was a long way. Every few feet, there was a translucent panel overhead, which let in enough light for her to see the endless spiral up ahead. She felt herself begin to panic. Perhaps she'd always be inside this slide. Or some idiot Librae might need the hospital and come racing down at thirty miles per hour, sending Astrid flying back down again, into the arms of the police. Or the slide itself would disappear and she'd fall with a splat.

Just as she had convinced herself that the slide was fading into nonexistence around her, it spat her out into the shrieking excitement of the Fourth Flower.

Astrid lay face down on the moss near the swimming pool until she'd caught her breath, her heart hammering. She'd escaped. A surge of excitement flooded through her.

She was home, in London Overhead.

15

Astrid got to her feet and hurried outside, limbs shaking with adrenaline. London Overhead was vivid and shimmering in the midday sun. A few Librae dotted the skies. Down below, blue lights strobed around St Thomas' Hospital, half hidden beneath the tree leaves.

They were hunting for her. Frantic. She was no longer just a missing child, either. She was a link to five others. Five other missing children.

What kind of Librae would do this? Steal children from the city below? And why?

The Librae had targeted a certain type of child. Children who weren't well cared for, who survived by the skin of their teeth. Their parents would struggle to mount a social media campaign, or lead a press conference. Their children might not even be reported missing. But that didn't mean they didn't matter.

Astrid hastened over the bridges. She could hear something up ahead, a noise coming from Fenchurch Tent. It took her a moment to recognise the sound as shouting, and a moment more to realise that Pent was the shouter.

'. . . have to help her! No one wants to take responsibility, and Finifugal won't let me in his stupid office, but you've been sending all of us down into London Underfoot unsupervised. Something was bound to happen, and now it has! We've got to do something!'

'Pent!' Astrid called.

Pent turned, and her face lit up.

'Astrid!' she shrieked, and she was running at her, and for the first time, Astrid was clasped in the arms of someone who wasn't her mother. Pent was clinging to her so tightly that it almost hurt, and sobbing wildly on her shoulder, and laughing, too.

'Where on earth have you been?' she said. 'Tristopher said the police took you away! I gave him a piece of my mind!'

Merchant Abebe came up and put a hand on Astrid's shoulder.

'I'm glad you're all right,' he said soberly.

Astrid opened her mouth, but Merchant Abebe had finally gathered his senses enough to say authoritatively, 'You ought to have informed me that the police in London Underfoot were looking for you. I'm reassigning you to shelving supplies.'

'And me too!' Pent said.

'Fine,' Merchant Abebe said.

'Look, I think Astrid and I deserve the rest of the day off. This has been hard on us both.' She flashed Astrid a grin.

'I think not,' Merchant Abebe said. 'Follow me, if you please.'

Pent sighed, and they obeyed.

'What a twit,' Pent said quietly, but not that quietly – Astrid watched Merchant Abebe's shoulders stiffen. 'He was all vague and useless. *The girl's gone home to her mother. An entirely predictable sequence of events. Don't give her another thought.* As if you would leave like that, without saying goodbye.'

'I wouldn't,' Astrid said. 'I know I said, before . . . I know I said I wanted to go home. But this is my home now.'

Pent put an arm around her.

Merchant Abebe led them inside Fenchurch Tent, a pyramid-shaped tent with five floors. They climbed up to the top level on a rope ladder braided with fairy lights, passing mysterious shops that sold books, sweets and bonsai trees. Astrid noticed a flap that hung open in the wall behind a counter.

'What does that shop sell?' she asked, and Merchant Abebe reddened.

'It's not a shop,' he said. 'I'm one of those people who rather struggles with throwing things away. That's my junk emporium. I keep all sorts in there.'

'Do you think I could have a look?' Astrid asked.

'What for?'

'I'm trying to fix up some of the stairs and bridges around here,' Astrid said. 'So many planks missing, nails sticking out, broken steps. Slippery lichen. It's dangerous.'

Merchant Abebe looked at her with narrowed eyes. Then he said, 'I've got a small daughter myself. Six and a half. Of course, she's not allowed to wander, but once she's a little older . . .' He paused. 'Councillor Paulson's in charge of infrastructure, is he not?'

Astrid shrugged.

'Take anything you need when you've finished with work,' Merchant Abebe said curtly. 'I have some old rock-climbing kit. Help yourself to ropes and harnesses. Don't take any risks with your own safety, will you?'

'Thank you,' Astrid said.

They reached the top level of the tent.

'This is where we sell the art supplies for Rain Muster,'

Merchant Abebe said, gesturing around him. Empty jars sat on shelves and on the floor. Crates and boxes. Illuminated display cases with glass doors. Everything was clearly labelled.

'I'll have the boxes brought up here. Then I'd like you to put the contents on display. Remember the importance of aesthetics, and check the labels. Hop to it.'

Merchant Abebe opened a flap of fabric and flew off, and Astrid filled Pent in on everything that had happened while they unpacked the parcels of beads into glass jars.

Pent frowned when Astrid finished her story. 'Lucky they took you to St Thomas',' she said. 'Who'd you reckon would do something like that, though? Stealing Librae children, I mean.'

'Well,' Astrid said slowly, 'Finifugal's never been . . . well, he's been quite hard on us.'

Pent was sceptical. 'Doesn't make him a kidnapper, though. Unless . . . did the kidnapper have vulture wings?'

'Of course Finifugal would have vulture wings,' Astrid said, rolling her eyes. 'Typical of him.'

'Seriously, though. The kidnapper could have been any older Librae. Or someone in a big coat, like the police thought.'

'I just have a feeling,' Astrid said. 'Did I ever tell you about the time I found him trapping starlings in Arbour Square? He said he was going to experiment on them.'

'Obviously that's revolting, but a feeling isn't a fact,' Pent said.

'Yes, I know. It doesn't mean anything. I just – I just wonder if it was him.'

'I think you're barking up the wrong tree,' Pent said. 'Why on earth would Finifugal kidnap a bunch of children? What's the point? There's any number of us hanging around being forced to do child labour, and we're all way more accessible.' Astrid tried to interrupt, but Pent held up a hand. 'I'm not a fan of Finifugal, but wouldn't he just kidnap a Starminster student if he was looking to kidnap someone?'

'Most of the people here have parents to kick up a fuss if they disappeared.'

'The externals don't. *You* don't,' Pent pointed out.

'How insensitive,' Astrid said, with a grin, which faded quickly. 'You're right, though. I was scared no one would come for me when I was in the police car. I sort of thought Mrs Wairi would keep an eye on me. But I haven't seen her in weeks.'

'Obviously not. She works in London Underfoot, and breaking you out of a police car would be an excellent way for her to get arrested and sacked. She's never here except when she's dropping off another new student, anyway. I'm sure she'll visit for Rain Muster, though. Most Librae never miss a festival.'

'Did you tell her I was gone?'

Pent shook her head. 'I didn't know how to contact her. Should have thought to ask Daniel, actually. I know it probably felt like forever, but I only heard you'd been taken – what, forty minutes ago? You can't have been gone for more than an hour.'

Pent was right. It had felt like forever.

'Who's Daniel?'

'Mrs Wairi's son. He goes to Starminster. He must be fourteen or so. In Upper Flights, I think.'

'I think I should tell her about this whole thing. Children going missing.'

'I'm sure it's on the news.'

'She might have missed it. Five children gone, Pent.'

'You could speak to Councillor Paulson, maybe?'

'I suppose,' Astrid said slowly. She was fairly certain that Councillor Paulson would tell her to stop imagining things, even with the evidence of the starling conversation.

They had finished with the beads, which were now glittering up at them from the jars.

'I'll do the silver filings,' Pent said. 'Can you start putting the oil paints in their display case?'

'Scared of stains?'

Pent held up her hands, fingers still marked with sludgy green. 'That's right. And you seem less unlucky with paint, so I'll let you handle it, if you don't mind.'

The oil paint's case was designed perfectly, each display tube fitting satisfyingly into its slot, neatly ordered from red to violet, with all the rest of the stock stored underneath for purchase. Pent and Astrid passed the rest of the afternoon companionably together sorting out the art supplies, the silence tranquil.

Astrid couldn't stop thinking about Pent's friendship. She had looked for her. She'd tried to find Mr Finifugal. She'd even lost her temper, because she was worried about Astrid. Pent cared about her. It was the most marvellous feeling.

Practically worth being snatched by the police.

*   *   *

Once they were finished with three shelves, oil paints organised, silver sparkling wildly beneath beams of white light, paper, brushes, pens and other materials all artfully displayed and labelled, it was twilight and time to head back to the Fourth Flower. Astrid was bone-tired, her sight shifting and distorting.

Astrid stopped by Merchant Abebe's junk emporium to help herself to a few tools, a bag of nails and some planks, and Pent helped her carry them as far as Starminster, where they hugged and parted ways. On her way back to the Fourth Flower, Astrid stopped to repair a weak step, nailing a plank over the soft, rotten wood. The blue lights were still strobing distantly below as she hammered inexpertly until the step was safe.

She returned to the Fourth Flower, but couldn't fall asleep.

Poor Mama. It had been painful, hearing Mama's gentle, loving voice, like an embrace. Astrid couldn't imagine her mother, with hay falling out of her hair and her earthy Yorkshire accent, in London.

Astrid thought back to the initials carved into the Crow's Nest. Mama hadn't said anything about London Overhead – she hadn't said *I know where you've been*. Too much of a risk, on a phone belonging to the police, perhaps.

Mama must have had a proper reason for the rhubarb shed, for those years of loneliness. Obviously Astrid was a Librae, so she would have wings someday, and join other Librae as a custodian of the sky. Whatever that meant.

But it kept niggling at her, the question that she couldn't answer. The rhubarb shed had been a place filled with love. Mama *loved* her. So why would Mama want Astrid to miss everything London Overhead promised?

Astrid flung off her duvet and got up. No point in trying

to sleep with these maybes and possibilities spiralling through her mind. She'd be better off fixing some broken railings. She flipped through her notebook to find a section of the city that needed repairs, and found a note she'd written. *Swingle Swangle Stairs near Starminster – impassable, half the steps missing. Net beneath also looks a bit ratty.*

There was nothing she could do about the net. But she could hammer in a few planks to make it safer. She packed her harness and tools and went out into the night.

A flock of Upper Flight students was leaving Starminster. Astrid recognised Beatrix's pure-white swan wings. They moved into a single line and flew northwards, the motion of their wings in perfect synchronicity.

Astrid stopped to watch them, longing in her heart. Lucky them. Lucky Fred Moutts, whom Pent had reported had been readmitted to Starminster. She'd heard from several sources that he had the wings of a greater spotted woodpecker. Everyone was obsessed with wing variants, and she was beginning to understand it, fantasising about the wings she might one day grow.

But flight had never felt so distant, and plodding along in her uncomfortable shoes, she felt like a different species to those Librae, and their elegant dominance of the sky.

She tied a rope to an industrial metal bridge and attached her harness to it before she took her first steps onto Swingle Swangle Stairs, which gave a worrying shudder.

After she'd nailed a few planks, Astrid came to the irritating realisation that she would need more than wood and nails to fix this staircase. There was something wrong structurally, and the stairs shook even more as she retreated back up to the safety of the metal bridge.

Someone was flying overhead, a shadow passing swiftly over Astrid. She looked up instinctively and saw a boy with enormous wings, twice as wide as his own height. He spotted her and gave a wave, then wheeled around and landed nearby.

Only then did Astrid recognise Mason.

'Your wings!' she blurted. 'When did you . . . ?'

'This morning. Not long after I saw you up at the Walkie-Talkie,' Mason said with a grin. He'd always come across as easy-going, but now, his wings folded and his shoulders relaxed, his joy was radiant.

'Look at you go! I thought you had to take lessons in Starminster before you could fly on your own.'

Mason shrugged. 'Looks like I'm just a natural.'

Astrid smiled. 'What kind of wings are they?'

'Peregrine falcon,' Mason said, pride written on his freckled face. 'Lucky, too. I'm the laziest Librae there is, so I was hoping for minimal flapping and fuss.'

'Congratulations,' Astrid said, hoping that was an appropriate word. 'What does it . . . flying. What does it feel like?'

'Better than anything. Better than eating good food, or talking to a friend.' He laughed, a wild infectious laugh that had Astrid laughing too, though he'd said nothing funny. 'I've never felt so . . .' He spread his wings. 'So free.'

'They're beautiful,' Astrid said, admiring their intricate pattern.

'I prefer *handsome*,' Mason said. 'What are you up to, anyway? Shouldn't you be asleep?'

'I'm trying to fix these stairs,' Astrid said. 'This place is dangerous. For those of us without wings, I mean.'

'Good call,' Mason said, nodding. 'Listen, I heard the police found you. Glad you're okay.'

'Thanks,' Astrid said. 'It was . . . weird.'

'Why did they pick you up, anyway?'

'Well,' Astrid said, 'to be honest, I'm sort of a missing child.'

'What? Did Mrs Wairi not check with your parents before she took you? She checked with mine. Took them all of twenty seconds to agree to shunt me off to boarding school. They were thrilled to get rid of me.'

'The police said some other children have disappeared and it looks like a Librae took them,' Astrid said. 'I think something strange is going on.'

'I wouldn't worry, Astrid,' Mason said cheerily. 'Let the adults take care of it.'

It was obvious that nothing could dim Mason's happiness. He rolled his shoulders, looking anxiously at Astrid.

'Oh, go ahead!' she said, laughing. 'I can tell you're itching to fly.'

'Sorry!' he said, flapping twice. He hovered above her for a moment. 'Maybe I could help with the repair work?'

'Don't be silly! Go enjoy your wings!'

'Thanks, Astrid!'

He flew away, his wings sending great flurries of air at Astrid. Envy caught at her again, and she pushed it away. Look how happy Mason was. She tried to share in his joy, tried to imagine her own future wings, refusing to allow herself to sink into self-pity.

Giving up on Swingle Swangle Staircase, Astrid untied her harness and walked towards Starminster, drawn towards the cathedral. Mr Finifugal had said that they couldn't go inside, but that didn't mean she wasn't allowed to look at the exterior.

She didn't take the usual mossy steps down to the Stone

Gallery. Instead, she veered off onto a wonky brick staircase that dumped her off at one of Starminster's bell towers. She peered through the pillars and saw a bell, gleaming in the darkness.

She scrambled down onto the roof. It was clearly designed with the need for regular maintenance in mind, with several walkways, which all looked significantly more secure than much of London Overhead.

Astrid was struck by the love invested in every stone of Starminster. Even these parts of the structure, which would surely have been seen by few, exhibited such craftsmanship, such thought. She kept encountering statues; the lead roofing was scrubbed clean, with dates and initials carved into it. Some were centuries old.

She walked along the edge of the roof, picturing the beauty of the cathedral below her feet. It felt long ago now, and she could hardly remember how it had looked. The details had faded into an indistinct blur of white-and-gold, the faces of stone angels watching soberly, fruit and flowers blooming in stone and wood and metal.

Starminster didn't look new, but it didn't look old, either. It was timeless. Infinite. Eternal.

She found a little nook in the gully of the roof where bird

feathers, dead leaves and old nests had accumulated, and sat down. It was sheltered from the wind, and also from the lights of London Underfoot. It took a while for her eyes to adjust, but eventually, she could pick a few stars out from the light-stained sky.

Astrid didn't intend to fall asleep, but it seemed that only moments later, dawn crept onto the sky, and she awoke, damp with dew.

16

Astrid started the day with a soak at one of the bathrooms. Then she trudged to Fenchurch Tent, where she and Pent continued to unpack boxes.

Pent had nipped to the loo when Astrid made her mistake. She reached for the highest box on a tower of others, and underestimated its weight. It slipped from her hands, crashing to the floor.

'Drat and blast it!' Astrid said, realising after it had slipped out that she was quoting Mama's favourite exclamation.

She ripped the box open.

Stained glass in rainbow colours, like a puddle of oil. It had been in perfect stacks, organised, and a backlit shelf was ready to display the glass. Now it was a box full of smithereens, a gleaming and dangerous mess.

Merchant Abebe appeared at the top of the ladder, with Pent just behind.

Pent took in the scene, and said immediately, 'Poor Astrid! A nasty accident. Which is, of course, the price you pay when you use child labour.'

'Thank you for that unnecessary remark, Penelope,' Merchant Abebe said. 'I was just on my way to pick up that box. The Headmaster passed by this morning to inspect our progress, and felt that its contents are not up to scratch.' He raised his eyebrows. 'They certainly aren't *now*. Tape it up again, Astrid, if you please. I'll be returning it to my supplier down in London Underfoot shortly.'

He flapped away as Astrid retrieved the tape. They closed the box, and then Pent said, 'Hold on.'

'What?'

Pent opened it. 'Odd,' she muttered. 'I could have sworn I saw . . .'

'What?'

'An envelope.'

Astrid shrugged, then gave the box a shake. It jingled, and then she saw it. An envelope, right at the bottom.

She reached into the box. Pent grabbed her wrist. 'Are you insane? Use tongs, at least.'

They dug around with tongs until Astrid snagged the envelope, waving it triumphantly. Pent ripped it open, eagerly unfolding the note inside.

Then she made a face and stuffed it back into the envelope. 'Nothing of interest.'

'Let me see.'

The note read like a jumble of nonsense words. *pykrete chambers. prepare equipment. 13 9.*

'Hm,' Astrid said. 'Are you thinking what I'm thinking?'

'Are you thinking *secret code*? Because if so, I already thought that and then dismissed it. And I know what you're going to say.'

'What?'

'That it's something to do with Finifugal, who you've decided is not only a bit uptight, but also a kidnapper.'

Astrid shrugged. 'Well, yeah. Merchant Abebe said the Headmaster was here today, looking at this glass. And the number could be . . . the date. Thirteenth of September is next week.'

'I wouldn't jump to conclusions. You strike me as someone who's crying out for a good conspiracy theory, Astrid. I bet you believe in the Loch Ness Monster.'

'There's some compelling evidence for Nessie,' Astrid retorted.

'Whatever,' Pent said, rolling her eyes and grinning.

The note abandoned, they found a rhythm, and Astrid began to enjoy the process – glass beads filling up tiny jars, plastic sacks of silver clay stacked in pyramids, tools laid out on embroidered cloth. Merchant Abebe came and took the box of fragments to be delivered back to London Underfoot.

But Astrid found it difficult to focus on their work with those five children on her mind. It niggled at her – the choice of those particular children. *Children from difficult backgrounds.* Someone had assumed they wouldn't be missed, that they weren't valued. And Astrid couldn't bear the thought of those forgotten children, in danger.

* * *

That evening at sunset, Astrid went to the Tenth Flower.

The skies were quiet as she walked, keeping an eye out for hazards. She hammered in the odd protruding nail, and scrubbed off some of the slippery moss with a wire brush. One bridge was so unsafe that she donned the harness that Merchant Abebe had given her, clipping herself onto the least rotten railing and trying to patch up some of the more dangerous holes. As she came closer to the Tenth Flower, she glimpsed Mr Barker, with his unkempt white mane and unkempt white

171

wings, leaving one of the staff apartments and heading for Starminster. She wondered what he would teach his students today.

When she reached the platform, the silhouette of the verbena towered over her like a many-headed gorgon. Astrid climbed aboard the lift. She pressed the button marked FINIFUGAL, heart pounding.

Her plan was a vague sketch at best. She wanted to get into Mr Finifugal's apartment, and take a look around. If five struggling children had passed through it, surely they would have left evidence somewhere.

She tapped the FINIFUGAL button again. The lift did not move.

Then she spotted the button a few names below: STRANGLEY.

He was probably teaching, too. Besides, she wasn't supposed to communicate with Starminster staff. Mr Finifugal had made that clear. He had threatened further discipline. Fred had toed the line, and had been readmitted to Starminster once he had fledged; maybe she would, too, so long as she didn't make more trouble.

But she wanted to see Mr Strangley again. If she explained about the missing children, he might be able to help. Mr

Finifugal would never know. Perhaps he hadn't left yet. It was worth a try.

She pushed the button for Mr Strangley and waited.

The lift began to rise.

When the doors slid open, Mr Strangley was waiting. He looked at her, his expression bland. 'Hello,' he said. 'I'm afraid I don't recall your name. You're one of our unfledged outcasts, I believe?'

'Astrid.'

'Of course.' He stood back from the lift and ushered her in. Astrid stepped inside, squinting in the sudden piercing light.

Three walls of his office were panelled with dark, shining wood and dotted with watercolour paintings, but one entire wall was glass, and the enormous window stood ajar. The room was filled with fresh air. Outside, Astrid could see a tiny balcony garden, the flowers golden in the light of the setting sun.

'I do feel responsible, you know,' Mr Strangley said, as though they had been in the middle of conversation. He said casually over his shoulder, 'Tea?'

'Yes, please,' Astrid said.

He went on as he walked into a small kitchen, in which everything was white: counters, cupboards, crockery. 'I encouraged you to rebel, and naturally, you did. I should have anticipated Finifugal's reaction.'

'We made our own choices,' Astrid said.

'In part. But I wound you up like clockwork toys, and I should have supported you in the Assembly.'

She was drawn to the fervour in his voice. And the regret. It was true. It hadn't occurred to any of them to rebel until he had presented it as an option.

'A brief and dramatic Assembly. Though I must admit, I've always enjoyed an Assembly at Starminster. "Jerusalem"! You know the poem, I assume?'

'No,' Astrid said.

Mr Strangley handed her a mug of tea and pointed at a framed print on his wall. She walked over and read the poem, taking a sip. The tea was sweet and strong, just how she liked it.

'It fascinates me, as a choice for Starminster's school song.' He sang in a deep tenor. '*And was Jerusalem builded here/Among these dark Satanic mills?*' He laughed. 'That horror of technological advancement! How apt, for our Overlords, with their superstitious desperation to keep all technology out of the city. The metaphorical mills of smartphones, of knowledge itself.'

It occurred to Astrid that Mr Strangley rather liked the sound of his own voice. 'It's just a song,' she said.

'Nothing is ever just a song,' Mr Strangley said, taking a gulp of his own tea. 'Everything is a choice.'

'Are you saying that Librae are . . . angels?'

'Aren't we?' Mr Strangley said.

'Of course not,' Astrid said stiffly.

Mr Strangley chuckled gently. 'Why have you come here today, Astrid?' he asked.

Astrid looked back into the solemn eyes of the teacher. 'Mr Strangley,' she said, 'have you heard children's voices in the Tenth Flower?'

Mr Strangley shook his head slowly. 'There are no children here but Nina Warburton, who lives with her mother. Why do you ask?'

Astrid deflected.

'Do you have a key to Mr Finifugal's apartment?'

His eyebrows shot up. 'What a very odd question. I don't, but even if I did, I certainly wouldn't be giving it to a student. Now be frank, Astrid. Is there something that you want to say?'

'Five children have been kidnapped in London Underfoot,' Astrid said. 'They say the kidnapper was a man with wings. And Mr Finifugal . . . did you know he traps starlings, and experiments on them?'

Mr Strangley was silent for a long time, his mug still halfway to his lips. Then he put down the mug, and said, 'Leave it with me. I'll investigate.'

'Thank you,' Astrid said.

'I'll speak to Councillor Paulson. He's in charge of infrastructure and immigration, as you may know. Not the most competent chap I've ever met, but he knows when people cross the borders.'

Astrid nodded.

'Don't take this as some kind of acknowledgement that your suspicions are correct,' Mr Strangley added. 'The notion that an Overheader, let alone Ferguson Finifugal, has kidnapped and concealed five children is extraordinarily unlikely. But in that unlikely scenario, great and lasting harm could ensue, so it is worthy of investigation.'

'Thank you, Mr Strangley.'

'Keep an open mind, Astrid. Not everyone is quite as they appear to be,' he counselled.

Astrid nodded again.

'You said earlier that Librae aren't angels,' Mr Strangley said.

'Well, they're not,' Astrid said. 'Are they?'

'You haven't fledged,' Mr Strangley said. 'Perhaps your opinion will change, when you take to the skies and watch the world shrink beneath you. You'll feel the blue of heaven tugging at you, and perhaps you'll come to realise that you are the closest living creature in history to an angel. The truth of the matter is that none of us knows what we are. We're mysteries, even to ourselves. Why should the month of our birth change our nature? Why do we gain the wings of different bird species, yet lack a bird's instincts so entirely? We know so little, and only science can answer our questions.'

Astrid said quietly, 'I feel like you're trying to tell me something.'

Mr Strangley laughed. 'I am,' he said. 'And you caught on immediately! Finifugal is unlikeable, prickly and – as you have discovered – a little too keen on experimenting with birds. But is he wrong? You have decided that he's rather malevolent, and perhaps your cohort agrees. Yet he's right about our profound ignorance about the Librae body, and he's trying to develop something, though I've no idea what. A theory, maybe. A textbook. The fundamental question is this: aren't the wings of Librae worth more than a few starlings?'

Astrid stared into the murky depths of her tea. Was Mr Strangley right? Was she overreacting to Mr Finifugal because she hated the idea of him experimenting on birds – especially when she had spent a lifetime without ever seeing a flight-gifted creature?

Birds must be dying in their dozens every day, down in London Underfoot. Cars obliterated them in a puff of feathers; cats sank sharp teeth into their breasts; sickness claimed them whole. So it made no sense for Astrid to feel so strongly about the Headmaster. And yet she couldn't talk herself out of it. She was certain that Mr Finifugal had taken the children from London Underfoot.

'I appreciate your help,' Astrid said. Without her noticing it, Mr Strangley had gently steered her back to the lift door. She handed him the mug. 'And thanks for the tea. It was just right.'

'I've always been told I made good tea,' Mr Strangley said, smiling.

A gentle chime, and the button next to the lift illuminated. 'That's odd,' he said. 'I didn't call the lift.'

The doors slid open. Mr Finifugal stood inside, his arms crossed.

Astrid felt sweat bead on her forehead, yet somehow, at the same time, she was suddenly extraordinarily cold.

'Strangley,' Mr Finifugal said, 'what a surprise to see you have this student here – stirring things up again?'

'We were merely having a cup of tea, Headmaster,' Mr Strangley said.

'I don't think a cup of tea will fly as an excuse. I'll speak with you later. Into the lift with you, girl.'

Astrid walked into the lift, her feet heavy as cement. The doors closed, and the last thing she saw was Mr Strangley's anxious face. Then she was alone with the Headmaster.

'I'm sorry,' Astrid said. 'I didn't—'

'I haven't got time for this,' Finifugal said, and his voice shook. For a moment, Astrid thought she saw a wet glint in his eyes. 'I've got more to worry about than just you, girl. And I'm running out of time.'

The lift doors opened again. Astrid's vision swam, and sweat rivered down her spine as she stared at the shining white tiles of a laboratory.

17

Mr Finifugal led Astrid into the laboratory. Astrid hardly dared look around, fearful that a bird might lie dead on the table, but there was no spot of colour in the glaring whiteness.

'Wait here,' Mr Finifugal said, and disappeared through a door.

It was cold in the laboratory. Her breath fogged – quick frightened puffs.

Surely Mr Finifugal wouldn't harm her.

Then again, if he'd kidnapped five children, what on earth would stop him?

That was the reason she'd come to the Tenth Flower in the first place, though. To check if he had kidnapped those children. She had hoped for just this – a moment when she could look for clues.

She began hurrying around, eyes darting over the surfaces. She peered into a refrigerator and found a few small vials, carefully labelled. She read the words *stem cells pigeon* and *stem cells house sparrow*. She had only a vague idea of what stem cells were, gleaned from her advanced biology programme back in the rhubarb shed. *The building blocks of life*, capable of turning into any type of cell. Scientists were still studying their possibilities.

But all this had nothing to do with five children vanishing.

Astrid heaved open a chest freezer, only to back away. It was filled with bird wings of dozens of species – tiny brown sparrow wings, raven wings as black as Pent's hair, starling wings with their starry constellations, wrapped in plastic. She shuddered and slammed it shut.

Footsteps.

She backed away from the freezer as Mr Finifugal came through the door. He held a struggling pigeon in his hands. Astrid noticed, with a quake of nausea, that it only had a single leg, a scrap of paper tied to it.

'I've banned you from Starminster,' Mr Finifugal said as he crossed the room. 'I've banned you from speaking to staff and students. I've sent all of you down into London Underfoot to fetch and carry. Yet that, it seems, is insufficient.'

Astrid said nothing.

'It may interest you to learn that six students in your cohort have recently fledged. It is often thus – as though fledging is contagious.' The pigeon gave a brief, spasmodic jerk. 'Nevertheless, every member of your cohort, fledged and unfledged alike, will be removed from their homes and confined here separately in unused staff quarters until further notice. You alone will continue to prepare for Rain Muster in Fenchurch Tent.'

'That's not fair!' Astrid forced her next words out. 'I'm the one who disobeyed – punish me!'

Mr Finifugal smiled. 'Rest assured. Your new friends will know that your disobedience is to blame for their punishment. You know isolation – you know what they will feel.'

'Please,' Astrid said, barely a breath.

Mr Finifugal opened the window. 'This pigeon will carry my message to Starminster, and the students will be removed immediately.'

He opened his hands, and the pigeon dropped a few feet before it flapped in the direction of Starminster. Astrid watched it go, her mouth dry.

Pent would be taken away from her family. Mason and Fred and the other recently fledged Librae had barely tried out their wings, and now they'd be locked up. Tristopher, Liane and Rick and Clair and Bethany. And they would know it was Astrid's fault.

She started to cry.

'Leave,' Mr Finifugal said.

* * *

Back out in London Overhead, it was now a damp and foggy evening, and cold. Astrid went to the Eleventh Flower to try to find Pent, but her nesthome was empty. She checked Fenchurch Tent. No Pent.

Astrid dragged herself, exhausted, back to the Fourth Flower, where the rumours were already flying. Sitting by the pool, eating lunch, a girl was saying, 'And he came into our lesson and took all the newbies! Said they had to come with him. They're going into, would you believe, *solitary confinement* because someone called Astrid broke the rules.'

'Why on earth didn't they refuse to go?'

'I think the te Strakas kicked off when they came for Tristopher. But the constables told them that if they didn't give him up, every te Straka would be kicked out of Starminster. I don't think that lad Mason, the one with the peregrine falcon wings, would have gone, but Finifugal had the constables put a wing-lock on him.'

Astrid flinched, hating the thought of Mason confined, his pristine wings locked away. She remembered painfully the infectious happiness on his face when he'd got them. How would he ever forgive her for this?

'Whoever Astrid is,' the other girl said, 'she'd better watch out. I'd have never taken that. Locked up with my brand-new wings for something I didn't do? I don't think so.'

With a jolt, Astrid recognised Beatrix. The Head Girl.

'Who is she, anyway? I've never heard of her.'

Astrid turned and hurried away, head low so that her hair covered her face.

Mr Finifugal had acted fast.

Pent would never hear Astrid's apology.

Back in her bubble, Astrid sobbed alone. She remembered the days of misery when Mama had caught the flu, and wouldn't visit to avoid infecting Astrid, leaving her meals just inside the door before beating a hasty retreat. Every hour had brought her closer to madness – her words, her *self*, dissolving into nothing.

As though she had ceased to exist.

* * *

Morning dawned without sleep, and Astrid walked, slowly and miserably, to Fenchurch Tent.

Merchant Abebe wasn't there, and she climbed up the rope ladders alone, remembering how she'd swung on them just yesterday with Pent. The top floor was half magnificent and half pure mess.

She opened a box and began to unpack the charcoal pencils within into their jars.

Two hours of unpacking and organisation later, Astrid was dejected and tired. When Pent had been here, they had chatted – admired their work – argued about how to display pastels or mahogany planks or swathes of oiled silk. Alone, the work felt tedious and seemed to take much longer.

When Merchant Abebe passed by to check on her, Astrid asked if he had ordered the new delivery of stained glass. 'I can go down and get it,' she offered. The tent was beginning to feel claustrophobically small and airless.

'Don't be ridiculous,' Merchant Abebe said with a snort. 'You're in enough trouble.'

'It's not fair,' Astrid said, unable to stifle a sob.

'Perhaps not,' Merchant Abebe said. 'But the headship at Starminster is a powerful role. Starminster is its own little world, and Mr Finifugal is the axle around which it all revolves. People need their children to be safe in Starminster, learning to fly in controlled conditions, and they'll accept whatever medieval punishment the fellow doles out if it means their young people are still educated at Starminster.' He paused for a moment, and Astrid thought his face softened slightly. He nodded to a stack of boxes behind her. 'I have already collected the replacement glass, and I will not mention the breakage to Mr Finifugal.'

'Thanks,' Astrid muttered.

'Finish off these shelves, and we'll call it a day, shall we?'

Astrid nodded. She started on the boxes of stained glass, lifting each piece carefully and slotting it into the backlit shelf. When she'd finished, they were throwing coloured shadows onto the walls of the tent.

She remembered the note they'd found in the box yesterday. She hunted for it in the mess of discarded packing materials, but couldn't find it.

It didn't matter. It was inscribed on her memory.

pykrete chambers. prepare equipment. 13 9.

What was *pykrete*?

Suddenly furious with herself, Astrid took a shaky breath. Her idiotic meddling was to blame for everything that had happened. Pent, locked in a room away from her family. All the people she'd started to befriend – people who'd shared a smile with her, laughed at her jokes – were imprisoned, their wings unused, alone. Because of Astrid.

Who gave a toss about pykrete chambers and enigmatic dates? Forget it. Forget it all. She was inventing a mystery where there clearly wasn't one. She owed it to Pent – to all of them – to do her job and keep her head under the parapet.

Maybe one day they'd forgive her.

*   *   *

Days dragged by. Astrid worked, then returned to the Fourth Flower, Pent's hat covering her hair. She didn't want to be recognised. There might be siblings after her, looking for revenge. Her dreams were always dark and bewildering, and when she awoke, her throat hurt as though she had been crying out in her sleep.

A week had passed, and the Fourth Flower was unusually quiet when she left her bubble. Not a single Librae flying overhead, and no one in the pool. Astrid yawned as she walked out into the city. On her way to Fenchurch Tent, she spotted a Librae flying alone in the dawn light, the outer feathers of his wings the deep blue of lapis lazuli, the inner as vividly turquoise as a tropical ocean. It was unusual to see a Librae with such flamboyant wings . . . like Mrs Wairi's.

It was half recognition and half instinct, but she raised her hand to the sky, and shouted, 'Daniel!'

The boy checked his flight at once, and corkscrewed down to Astrid. He looked as though he weighed nothing, as though gravity had no power over his body.

She thought, wistfully, of her own future wings.

But even fledging couldn't fix what she'd done.

The boy landed on the bridge.

'Daniel Wairi?' Astrid said.

'That's me.' He looked at her curiously. 'Let me guess. Another of my mother's acquisitions.'

Astrid nodded.

'There are rather a lot of you running around,' Daniel said, his voice flat.

'I'm looking for her,' Astrid said. 'For Mrs Wairi.'

'You're not the only one,' Daniel said. His wings opened. 'I can't help you.'

'Please!' Astrid said. 'Listen to me. Have you heard about the unfledged cohort?'

'I heard they're locked up,' Daniel said, with a shrug. 'Finifugal is a law unto himself. I would stay far away from him, if I were you.'

'Surely he can't just lock people up! Can't your mum help?'

Daniel shook his head. 'My mum doesn't interfere with matters at Starminster. She's got enough to occupy her.' He ruffled his feathers and spread his wings wide, enveloping Astrid in a vista of blues.

'I don't have anyone else to help me,' Astrid said. It was hard to speak through the lump in her throat. 'I don't have anyone.'

'I told you,' Daniel said, his voice now almost a shout, 'I can't help you.'

He took off, those remarkable indigo-turquoise wings shining as though every plume were varnished, and Astrid watched him fly until she couldn't see him any more.

So Mrs Wairi couldn't help. Mr Strangley had said he would ask around, but for all she knew, he'd been sacked.

Numbness stole over her, dimming her vision as she walked over the bridges that had become so familiar beneath her feet.

When she reached Fenchurch Tent, Merchant Abebe greeted her chipperly. 'Have you heard the news?'

'What news?' Astrid said dully.

'Rain is forecast!' Merchant Abebe said. She almost expected him to perform an excited jig. 'Rain Muster is imminent. I'm going to open the art-supply shop later on today, and I'll assist you with the remaining shelves.'

Astrid had been looking forward to Rain Muster – the song,

the weird and gorgeous art, visiting the Hanging Gardens for the first time. Pent had told her about the different levels and their circulating flowers, changing with every season.

She wouldn't be attending now. The Hanging Gardens would be full of people who hated her – Pent's parents, the te Strakas, Starminster students, Mr Finifugal.

All that day, she worked under the beady eye of Merchant Abebe.

'Do people not already own art supplies?' she asked.

'I forget how ignorant externals are,' Merchant Abebe said breezily. Somehow, it felt more insulting from him than from Pent. 'No. There's a time limit – that's part of the competition. Though I'm certain some people will have been planning their pieces for a long time. Anything that's left over will be made into smaller pieces and sold at cost.'

They finished late that evening. Astrid lit the hundreds of candles with long tapers and Merchant Abebe switched on the lights. He tied back one of the cloth walls, so that the Librae customers could fly directly into the store.

'Be a bit awkward if it all burst into flame,' Astrid observed.

'The tent is flameproof!' Merchant Abebe said. He was trying to scowl, but a wide grin was breaking through his usual scepticism.

Astrid could see why.

The shop glowed. Every object looked gilded, precious. Astrid felt a swell of pride. She was a cog in the workings of London Overhead, however tiny. She had contributed to Rain Muster. She belonged here.

The pride was followed by excruciating guilt.

Pent should be here. All of them should. All of them had carried heavy loads so that the exhibits for Rain Muster would be complete.

'Thank you for your hard work, Astrid,' Merchant Abebe said. 'Hopefully the current state of affairs won't continue for long. I've been informed that you will be working elsewhere from tomorrow.'

'Where?' Astrid said.

'I'm not sure. But, look. Best of luck, eh? With all of this, and with the repairs. It's a fine idea.'

Astrid thanked him and shook his hand. She climbed back down the rope ladders, weary, sad.

Someone stood at the entrance to the tent, wings extended, a dark silhouette against the coral-coloured, light-polluted sky.

Mrs Wairi.

18

Mrs Wairi's arms enfolded Astrid as she sobbed out broken sentences. 'Children are . . . missing from London Underfoot, and then Mr Finifugal took my friends and locked them all up . . . because I was talking to Mr Strangley. And I found a message in a box that was supposed to be delivered to London Underfoot. It said *pykrete chambers. prepare equipment*, and a date, and the date was – it was today . . .'

'Slow down, Astrid. Delivered where in London Underfoot?'

Astrid gazed at her with a look of dawning horror. 'I don't . . . know.'

'Then put it out of your mind. It's irrelevant. Where is the Headmaster keeping your friends?'

'They're in the empty staff quarters. On the Tenth Flower.'

Mrs Wairi touched her cheek. 'You've been very brave. Be brave a little longer.'

Then she opened her wings and took to the skies, leaving Astrid standing at the threshold of Fenchurch Tent.

Above, Astrid could hear the flutter of Librae landing in the art-supply shop, their footsteps on the wooden platform, and faintly, the jingle of someone measuring out beads on the scale.

She began to follow Mrs Wairi on foot. The sky above was burgeoning with clouds, with not a single star visible. Yet she was enveloped with vast, whole-body relief. Mrs Wairi was an adult, and powerful. She had believed Astrid at once, acted at once.

By the time Astrid reached the Tenth Flower, spiky as a virus against the night, Librae were hovering around it, standing at the lift doors. When the lift began to move down from one of the upper blooms, she had to push through the crowd to see.

The lift doors opened, and Mrs Wairi stood in the centre of a knot of children.

'Pent,' Astrid said, and she ran towards her. Pent hugged her, but quickly let go. Her hair was tangled, and her face was marked with the salt stains of old tears.

Tristopher was there too, anxiety twisting his face. Rick, Gregory, Deborah and a couple of others.

But where was Mason? Fred, Clair, Liane? Bethany and Oliver?

Mrs Wairi wasn't smiling. Instead, she spoke to the crowd that had gathered outside the lift. 'Call the constables. At once.'

Several people took off immediately.

Pent's face was drawn.

'Where are the others?' Astrid whispered.

'Their rooms are empty.' Pent's voice was hoarse with disuse.

'We need to search the entire Tenth Flower,' Mrs Wairi was saying in a low, urgent voice to the Librae gathered around. 'A number of students are missing.'

'How many are we talking?'

'Six. All recent fledglings.'

'What about Finifugal?' Astrid called out.

'No sign of him either,' Mrs Wairi replied. She raised her voice again. 'We need to find the Headmaster. He must answer for this treatment of students, and tell us the location of the missing fledglings.'

'Half of the Overlords have conspired with this balderdash!' shouted Tristopher's father, who had just landed and had both arms wrapped around his son. 'I've been up in the Second Flower every day, begging to have Tristopher released. Finifugal's been permitted to run wild with our children!'

'You're right, Reginald,' Mrs Wairi said. 'This never should have happened. I've been needed in London Underfoot and only returned today when my son informed me of the situation. But we will deal with the past in the future. For now, we must focus on the missing children. The door from Finifugal's laboratory to his rooms is steel, and locked,' she continued. 'We're going to break it down.'

Pent and Astrid moved out of the way of the inrush of constables landing. Not long later, Councillor Paulson turned up with a blowtorch under his arm.

The constables, Councillor Paulson and Mrs Wairi piled into the lift. Just as the doors began to close, Astrid and Pent slipped inside too. When they reached the laboratory, no one noticed the children follow the adults as they filed into the lab. As Councillor Paulson prepared the blowtorch for action, Mrs Wairi said in a voice that was low with fury, 'How could you let this happen?'

'My dear Mrs Wairi!' sputtered Councillor Paulson.

'Don't you *dear* me. Finifugal's a difficult man, and we all know he's troubled. But to allow this?'

'I'm sure it's a misunderstanding. And I'll *allow* you to explain to Ferguson why his door's wrecked.'

A hiss emanated from the door as the blowtorch started its work, accompanied by the acrid stink of burning.

'With pleasure. I'll wreck more than his door before this is over.'

After a short while, the door gave way, and Mrs Wairi and Councillor Paulson stormed through along with the troop of constables.

Astrid squeezed Pent's hand. They followed.

But there was nothing to see – only ordinary rooms. A little impersonal, but nothing strange. A bathroom with a claw-footed tub. An office, with a picture of a smiling woman on the desk. A bedroom, still smelling of sleep, the bed unmade.

'They're not here,' Mrs Wairi said.

'What about—' Astrid said.

'Astrid! Pent!' Mrs Wairi snapped. 'What are you still doing here? This is no place for children.'

'Hang on, though,' Astrid said. 'What about – Tristopher said his house had stem cellars. Doesn't this place have stem cellars?'

Mrs Wairi and Councillor Paulson shared an uneasy look.

'She's right,' Mrs Wairi said. 'I think they're accessible from the lift. Is that correct, Paulson?'

'Yes,' Councillor Paulson said, fishing out a jingling set of keys. 'I have the emergency key right here.'

'And just think,' Mrs Wairi murmured to him as they went

back out towards the lift, 'we wouldn't have needed any of this if you'd exhibited a smidgen of common sense weeks ago.'

Astrid and Pent followed them back into the lift, but Mrs Wairi pressed the button for the main entrance and firmly directed them out. 'I mean it, Astrid,' she said. 'Take Pent home to her family.'

The doors shut.

'Pent, I'm sorry,' Astrid said. 'I should have taken you home. Are you okay? Are you – are you hungry or thirsty or anything? I'm so sorry that he did this to you.' She paused, and forced out her next words. 'It's all my fault. You must . . . you must hate me.'

Pent's eyes were huge and vacant in her face. 'It was really hard,' she said eventually, her voice slow and halting. 'Nothing bad happened, though. Nothing happened at all. For days. It was hard.'

'It's my fault,' Astrid repeated, shame writhing within her.

'Don't say that,' Pent said. 'You didn't lock me up. It was *his* fault. But, Astrid, there was something wrong with Finifugal.'

'He's horrible!'

'That's not what I mean. He was – he was crying. Crying like his heart would break.'

'Why?'

'I don't know. Not because of us. He didn't care about us at all. But I heard him twice, in the night, sobbing.'

'Are you sure it wasn't one of the others?'

'No. It was him.'

Astrid shook her head. 'I just – I don't understand. Listen, I've got to take you home, okay?'

'I was thinking about the message, while I was locked up. You know. *pykrete chambers. prepare equipment.* And the date. It's today's date, right? I think you—'

From the Tenth Flower, Astrid heard a whistle blowing. She turned and saw constables, swooping through the air in a neat V formation. One flew past, close enough to touch, and Pent caught at his uniform.

'What did you find?' she said urgently. 'What was in the stem cellars?'

'Nothing,' the constable said, flapping to stay aloft while tugging his jacket from Pent's grasp. 'But Finifugal had been keeping people in there. More than one, by the looks of the toilet bucket.'

'The children from London Underfoot,' Astrid said. 'I knew it – I knew it!'

The constable broke free and flew off, directing a nasty look at Astrid and Pent.

'Listen to me, Astrid,' Pent said doggedly. 'I was wrong about that message. You were right. It's got to be a code, something Finifugal was sending to someone in London Underfoot. The pykrete chambers. What are they?'

'I already told Mrs Wairi about this, and she said it was irrelevant,' Astrid said.

'She doesn't know Finifugal like we do. He might be a nutter, but he's single-minded. This was all planned right from the start. Locking us up – everything. So the pykrete must mean something.'

'But the note never made it to its destination anyway, did it? We took it out of the box, we threw it away.'

Pent swallowed.

'It did,' she said quietly.

'What do you mean?'

'I put it back in the box.' She hesitated. 'It just . . . I didn't want us to get in any more trouble. And I thought you were overreacting. But I was wrong. I'm sorry, Astrid.'

Astrid's mind raced, but she tried not to let Pent see any hint of panic on her face. 'Don't be sorry. It doesn't matter. Finifugal would have found a way to get the message wherever it was meant to go.'

'We've got to get to the pykrete chambers, whatever they

are. I know! The library.' Pent started to walk, but her pace lagged, as though she'd forgotten how to move quickly.

'Pent, I'm supposed to take you home. You need to rest, and your parents and Polly will be desperate to see you.'

'I can go home later,' Pent said. 'Come on.'

They were close to the Fourth Flower, and Pent was hurrying now, pulling at Astrid to keep up. 'The indigo slide goes to Starminster,' she panted.

The Fourth Flower was deserted, and they were at the mouth of the slide before Astrid had prepared herself. 'You go first,' she said to Pent.

'Not a chance,' said Pent, and gave her a push.

Astrid plunged into the mouth of the slide, a scream spilling out of her mouth as she rocketed down. By the time she shot out of the end, landing hard on hands and knees, she was so dizzy that the black and white tiles swam in her vision.

Pent slammed into her a moment later, knocking them both flat on their backs. For a second, they lay still, staring up at the golden mosaics of Starminster. 'Where are we, exactly?' Astrid said dazedly.

'The North Transept. Get up, Astrid.'

Pent was pulling at Astrid's hand.

'Come on,' she said. 'Hurry up! We'll be able to find pykrete in the library. Everything's in there.'

'Where is the library?'

Pent bared her teeth in a grisly smile. 'Christopher Wren's grave,' she said. 'Where else?'

There was another library, Pent explained between breaths as they rushed down the stairs towards the crypt, on the triforium level, musty and grand and useless for Starminster homework purposes. But the Hidden Library contained a treasure vault of Librae history.

'Barker would gladly die for it, I'm sure.'

'Was Christopher Wren a Librae? He designed this place, right?'

Pent shrugged. 'You'll have to ask Barker. I have no clue. It would be appropriate though, right? I can just imagine him with dainty little wren wings.'

Sir Christopher Wren was buried in a corner of the crypt. His memorial was a simple block of stone, obsidian-black, and Astrid paused to read his epitaph: '*Lector, si monumentum requiris, circumspice*. What does that mean?'

'Oh, I know this one,' Pent said. 'Barker gave us a tour at the beginning of the year, before you joined, and he said it meant, *Reader, if you seek his monument, look around.*'

'Clever clogs,' Astrid said, and Pent gave a mortified grimace.

She pressed down hard on the corner of the black stone for several seconds. Slowly, with a pneumatic hiss and a growl, the stone lifted.

Below it, instead of the bones of Christopher Wren, was a staircase.

Astrid and Pent went down the stairs into the darkness below.

When they reached the bottom, they stood on the cusp of a narrow bridge. It didn't have a handrail, and below it, the drop stretched down and down.

'This is beyond dangerous,' Astrid said. The shelves, with their wealth of literature, lined the pit. It was lit with golden electric bulbs, and a single walkway spiralled down, about the width of Astrid's shoulders. There was neither handrail nor net, and the floor was unforgiving stone tiles: a blurred star mosaic, the stone pitted and dark.

'Requires both nerve and balance,' Pent said. 'I've often thought that a few spatters of blood would add to the Gothic vibe.'

Astrid followed Pent over the bridge to the catalogue, which sat on a megalithic podium in the centre of the library, at the end of the bridge. A vast crystal chandelier twinkled above the catalogue. The library was deserted, and their voices echoed as though they were at the bottom of a well.

'*Pykrete*,' Pent said, flipping through the weighty pages with effort. 'Never heard of it – hope it's English, could be Greek . . .'

She ran her finger down the list of words, squinting. 'There! It's in a book called *Innovation during World War II*.'

They looked at each other. 'That's odd.'

'Better go check out the book,' Pent said, slamming the catalogue shut with a bang. 'It's about halfway down.'

It was slow going on the narrow walkway. At a couple of points, Astrid found her vision darkening at the edges again. But she kept on walking, one hand on the library's shelves, gathering a soft coating of dust.

At last, Pent pulled out a book with a brown leather spine. A puff of dust arose. She handed it to Astrid. Astrid checked the index, then turned to page 217, and read aloud:

'*Geoffrey Pyke's substance was simple: ice mixed with sawdust. It was believed that pykrete, with its unusual qualities such as a low melting point, could be used to build an enormous platform in the ocean, a man-made iceberg in essence, upon which British planes could safely land. In the cold chambers five floors below Smithfield Market, Pyke experimented on the substance . . .*'

Smithfield Market.

The children were in those cold chambers.

When Astrid looked at Pent, her hands were shaking. '*Prepare equipment*,' she whispered. 'What equipment?'

'It doesn't matter. We have to get there *now*,' Astrid said, sliding the book back.

They hurried back up the walkway, concentrating on the climb, but it still seemed to take twice as long. At one point, Pent's foot slid out from beneath her, and she windmilled her arms wildly. Astrid grabbed her hand and steadied her. They had to pause for a few seconds. Pent's hand was clammy. 'We have to hurry,' she said.

'Wait until you're steady,' Astrid urged.

When they finally emerged from the grave, Pent was breathing heavily, sweat on her face. 'I'm worn out,' she said. 'I suppose it makes you lose fitness, sitting for days in a room all by yourself.'

'Where is Smithfield Market?'

'It's a ten-minute walk,' Pent said. She pulled her notebook out of a pocket and opened it. She had to flick through dozens of pages before she found a blank one, where she started to draw a map. Astrid couldn't miss what was written, over and over again, in tiny text, on those pages. *I want my mum. I want my dad. I want my sister.* And she realised why Pent was drawing the map for her; she would not be coming too.

When Pent had finished, she handed it to Astrid. 'I know I shouldn't leave you,' she said, eyes full. 'And I want to come. I really do.' Her tears spilled over. 'I'm – I'm a terrible friend.'

'You're the best friend I've ever had,' Astrid said. 'Go home. Go see your parents. And besides, I need you. You've got to tell Mrs Wairi where I've gone. Ask her to come. And to bring help. I can't – I can't do this by myself.'

'I will,' Pent said. 'I promise.'

Pent showed her to a back exit – the gigantic main doors to St Paul's were long since shut and bolted.

'I'll see you soon.'

'Mrs Wairi will probably reach Smithfield before you do,' Pent said encouragingly.

Astrid shoved open the old door and went out into the night.

It was a glowering night, fog in the air, and chilly. She looked down at the map and began to walk, checking the street names against Pent's neat handwriting. Past Paternoster Square, the one she'd often seen from above.

Astrid kept her gaze away from the Underfooters and walked with purpose, as she'd practised when she'd been a courier collecting gold chips with Tristopher. That was how Underfooters walked. But she was an Overheader. She didn't want to be like these people, trapped in their maze with only fragments of sky, portioned out stingily, rare and precious.

She didn't want them to spot her, either. The missing girl, the key to the missing many.

On and on, around the curve of the Smithfield Rotunda Garden.

The long brick building in front of her, flanked by pale towers, must be Smithfield Market. Even though it was not yet dawn, the market was bustling with life – men in white coats were carrying plastic-wrapped carcasses through doors that threw out light.

For a second, she thought that a Librae was crouched on the roof looking down at her, and gave a terrified start. But it was just a statue.

Surely Mrs Wairi must be on her way?

She glanced up at the skies, but London Overhead was quiet and still.

Astrid needed to find a way into the old building without being seen. Luckily, a door nearby stood ajar. She pushed it open with a strident creak. She stood, frozen, for a second.

She didn't want to go inside Smithfield Market. She had never wanted anything less. There was a stench of farmhouse around these doors and a less familiar smell – the reek Mama brought to the rhubarb shed at slaughtering time.

But her friends were somewhere inside. Her cohort. And a group of children she didn't know, children who'd had difficult upbringings, children who Mr Finifugal believed would never be missed.

Astrid heaved the door open, and went inside, into a weighty darkness.

The door slammed shut behind her.

19

It took a moment for her eyes to adjust. But Astrid's eyes still functioned better in dim light than in bright, and soon, in the greenish glow of emergency exit signs, she could see.

Unlike the nearby market, this was a building site: an empty, echoing space, with a wide, arched ceiling disappearing into darkness. It was oddly splendid, and yet the reek lingered.

Astrid wasn't sure how to get to the chambers where pykrete had been developed. But it didn't matter. She knew where she was headed.

Down.

She tried every door, until she found a staircase.

Stairs, corridors, always downward. The temperature dropped as she moved deeper underground.

At last, she came to an ancient brick corridor. Designed, perhaps, by Horace Jones, more than a century ago.

Tons of earth and stone above her. The velvet darkness, kept at bay by the emergency exit sign's greenish light. Shadows reached from doorways, swaying living things. Out of sight, something was dripping rhythmically. She thought of the rhubarb shed, the sound of its growth. Of things moving beneath the surface, of pale worms pouring out of the soil.

A light shone faintly from the end of the corridor.

Astrid stopped, and pressed her palms against the brick, trying to calm her breathing. 'I can't do this,' she said aloud, and her words echoed, as though in confirmation.

She thought, again, of the kidnapped children. After days and days locked in the stem cellars of the Tenth Flower, they were underground, at the mercy of Mr Finifugal.

Astrid straightened her shoulders and smoothed down her hair. She crept towards the light.

She knew that Mr Finifugal would be at the other end, but he wasn't working alone. That mysterious message had been intended for someone. The location, the date. And the task: prepare equipment.

The whisper of Astrid's shoes on the brick was loud in her ears. She passed an emerald-green wrought-iron staircase to nowhere; she crept, slowly and cautiously, through a doorway and into a maze of passages.

Some of the walls glistened with dampness, and there were loose piles of bricks and odd trailing wires running through the hallways. Astrid picked her way over the uneven floor. She could see a glint of light up ahead, and she followed it until she rounded a corner.

In the beams of a spotlight, hospital beds, metal and white-sheeted. Two rows of six.

In the beds, twelve children.

They lay on their fronts. The Librae children's wings were open, spread on top of the sheets. Mason lay in the closest bed, his face furrowed and absent, and his new wings so wide that they cascaded onto the floor on either side of the bed.

Twelve children. That was odd.

She knew of five kidnapped from London Underfoot. And six newly fledged Librae taken from the Tenth Flower. Mason, Fred, Bethany, Clair, Liane and Oliver.

He must have kidnapped another child. Despite her suspicions, he'd come down and taken another.

Astrid moved closer. Then she noticed something strange.

A girl in the last bed was sitting up and reading a book. *Peter Pan.*

Astrid steeled herself, and stepped out into the pool of light.
Nothing happened. No one leapt from the shadows.

As Astrid came closer, the girl looked up, and started violently.

'It's okay,' Astrid said, holding up her hands. 'I'm here to
help you. Don't be scared. It's – I'm going to get you home,
okay? I know you must be feeling really . . . really scared. But
don't worry. Try to stay calm.'

The girl gaped at her, the book falling from her hands.

'What's your name?' Astrid said. 'I'm Astrid.'

'E-Elise,' the girl said.

'You're going to be okay, Elise.'

Bags of clear fluid were suspended next to each child. Tubes
ran down into a needle in the backs of their hands.

Was Mr Finifugal keeping them unconscious? What was his
plan?

Memories flashed in front of her eyes. Wings . . . wings.
Stem cells in the refrigerator, carefully labelled. Stem cells. The
building blocks of life.

She knew, in a burst of awareness, what Mr Finifugal was
planning.

He was going to remove their wings. And he was going to
use stem cells to graft them onto the backs of these other
children.

Astrid doubled over and retched.

To steal their wings – to cut them off –

Wings were what made them Librae. Without their wings, what were they? Not Librae any longer. How could they ever heal from that? The sky theirs, and then, in a second, the sky stolen from them forever.

A machine was whirring in the corner. Astrid peered into it. Rows of glittering scalpels.

Astrid ripped off the tape and pulled out Mason's IV. Then she did the same to the others, running from one child to the next, Overheaders and Underfooters alike, tearing at the strips of surgical tape, plucking out needles and flinging them on the floor.

Behind her, she heard a groan and a crash. Mason had fallen off his bed, which had rapidly transitioned him from unconscious to waking.

'What . . . ?'

Astrid pulled out the last two needles and rushed to Mason.

'What happened?' Mason slurred. His eyes were unfocused.

'It's okay,' Astrid said, fighting to keep her voice steady. 'You're awake now. Just give yourself a minute.'

Mason tried to rise, but his arms were too weak to support him, and he slumped forward instead, one unwieldy wing falling, cumbersome and itchy, on Astrid's shoulders.

The others were stirring. Clair, who she hardly knew, lay still, eyes wide, and Bethany was crying.

The children from London Underfoot were quicker to recover. One boy prodded at the puncture wound in his hand, then turned on Astrid with fury on his round cherubic face. 'What are you doing?' he demanded.

'What happened?' Oliver said, his voice croaky. 'Last thing I knew, I was eating dinner in the Tenth Flower.'

'It was Finifugal,' Astrid said. 'He brought you here.' She wavered, uncertain whether she should tell them Mr Finifugal's plans.

Clair spread her wings, too wide for them to possibly be mistaken for fakes. The non-Librae children gasped, and the Librae flinched as one as she tried to launch herself into the air.

'Stop, Clair – you're going to hurt yourself!' Mason said.

Clair crashed ten feet away, a nasty skid over the concrete floor, and landed with one wing trapped beneath her and the other ruffled. As Clair heaved herself to her feet, Astrid saw that her hands and knees were bleeding.

Fred winced. 'Flying,' he said. 'Not as easy as it looks.'

The kidnapped children gave a murmur of bewilderment. They were bunching together, gawping at the wings. One elbowed another, and said, 'What d'you reckon? Bad dream?'

'Don't try to fly!' Astrid cried. 'Just take a minute, okay?'

'He's coming,' Bethany said. She was sitting on the floor, her teal and orange kingfisher wings draped around her like a cloak.

Astrid moved into the cluster of Librae, and said in a low voice, 'You can't fly in front of these children. They'll think they're losing it. Besides, there's no way you could escape by flight. Finifugal's faster than any of you.'

Oliver, who had pale-pink jay wings with a stripe of vivid blue, said, 'Why were we in hospital beds?'

The girl who'd been reading the book, Elise, was the only child still sitting on the bed. Her knees were drawn up beneath her chin, eyes darting back and forth.

'What should we do?' Bethany said.

'We need to get out of here. Each Librae with an Underfooter. Run any way you can. Finifugal can't catch everyone if we're all going in different directions,' said Astrid.

Mason had climbed to his feet by this point, and nodded firmly.

Fred, who had risen carefully and sensibly, as he did everything, looked uneasily at the other children. 'Where should we take them?' he said.

'To the police,' Astrid said. 'Wings away and don't deploy them until these children are safe.'

The fledglings' wings disappeared as she spoke, the other children agape.

'I know it's scary, but we have to save them.' She paused before she spoke again, unsure whether to tell them what was going on. But she knew that she wouldn't want to be kept in the dark, would always rather know what was at risk. She spoke rapidly and brutally. 'Finifugal's going to take your wings if you don't get out of here.'

The Librae children paled. Mason reached out involuntarily and touched his back with one hand.

'We'll get further without the dead weight,' Oliver muttered, glancing over at the other children uneasily.

Mason turned on him, fists clenching. 'Don't call them that,' he snarled. 'Haven't you learned anything from what's happened to us? People are valuable whether they've got wings or not.'

A pugnacious expression appeared on Oliver's face. He looked as though he might square up to Mason. But a second of ferocious eye contact, and he subsided.

'Whatever,' he said. 'Fine. I'll risk my life and my wings for a stranger. Sure.'

'That's more like it, mate,' Mason said, clapping Oliver on the shoulder as if he'd spoken sincerely.

They looked to Astrid as though she was an authority, and

she did her best. 'Pair up,' she said. 'Mason, take the boy from the first bed, and Fred, see if you can haul along that girl with the book – her name's Elise.'

She turned to the children she didn't know. 'You're in danger. Hang on to your partner and do what they say, and they'll get you to safety,' she said.

The boy from the first bed opened his mouth, his belligerent expression only emphasised by the dimples in his cheeks. 'First of all, what's up with the costumes?' he demanded.

'Not now,' Astrid snapped. 'We're running out of time.'

'Astrid?' Fred said uneasily. 'She won't come.'

Astrid turned around, ready to tell him to drag Elise if he needed to, only to see that she was gripping the bed, and she had a phone in her hand, which was emitting a rhythmic sound.

She was phoning someone.

Every eye was drawn to the bright screen, and it rang once more, before a deep voice said, 'Elise?'

'You need to come,' said Elise into the phone, her voice shrill in the silent passage. 'They've all woken up. They're trying to run away.'

Astrid ran at Elise and snatched the phone from her hand, flinging it onto the stone floor with force. It smashed, glass flying.

'Why?' Mason shouted at Elise.

'Forget it! Leave her, Fred – go!'

Running footsteps, echoing in the corridor.

'He's coming,' Astrid said. 'Go! *Go!*'

They scattered. Mason and his partner headed in the opposite direction that Astrid had come from, and the others disappeared into the shadowed mouths of other passages. They were quickly out of sight.

Astrid legged it too, entirely on instinct, in the same direction as Mason. She'd only taken a couple of steps when she felt an unexpected hitch on her ankle, and toppled down, landing hard on elbows and knees.

It was Elise, her thin arms entwined around Astrid's ankle.

'Get off me!' Astrid shouted, tugging at her, but the girl's grip was incredibly strong.

'You've ruined everything!' Elise shrieked, her eyes bulging.

Astrid kicked out, hard, and connected with Elise's nose, which began to fountain blood. Before she could get up, Mr Finifugal burst into sight, his chest heaving.

For a moment, he took in the scene – then he saw Elise, and ran towards her, lifting her back onto her feet.

'Go to the office,' he said, 'and lock yourself in.'

Astrid scrambled up, and Elise gave her a last baleful glare before disappearing into the shadows.

Mr Finifugal made an awful sound that began as a wheezing wail and faded into something more like a sob.

'You,' he said, and lunged at Astrid.

Astrid backed away as fast as she could. She should run, but if she ran, what would prevent Mr Finifugal from picking off the nearest escapees? No one had gone far – she could still hear footsteps, and only ten feet ahead of her, Mason and his partner had frozen, utterly still.

If Mr Finifugal spotted them, he would deploy his own wings, and they'd be in his grasp in a second. He would take Mason's wings – Mason's resplendent wings, patterned like the ridges and runnels of a desert. He would use stem cells to paste them onto someone else.

'Why are you doing this?' Astrid said, raising her voice so that it echoed. 'They've done you no harm.'

'Where are the students?' Mr Finifugal growled. 'Where have they gone, girl?'

Mason and his partner were beginning to creep further into the darkness.

'You're planning to take their wings, aren't you?' Astrid shouted, her voice shaking, but loud enough to drown their footsteps. 'You're planning to use stem cells to stick them onto someone else's back. But why? What for?'

Mr Finifugal took another step closer. Grooves of shadow fragmented his face. He was weeping soundlessly, tears pouring down his cheeks, catching in the lines that bracketed his mouth.

I heard him twice, in the night, sobbing.

This wasn't just the failure of an experiment. This failure was something much worse to Mr Finifugal. A thousand times worse.

Why did Mr Finifugal care so much about this?

She'd missed something. She must have. And he was coming closer, and if she backed away much further, he'd be within feet of Mason and the boy.

Mr Finifugal flexed his fingers. Light caught on the gold ring that he wore on the fourth finger of his left hand.

Astrid saw it, and she remembered. Tristopher had mentioned it a long time ago, in the lift.

His wife's not a Librae.

'Your wife,' she said. 'You want wings for your wife.'

He paused for a second, surprise flashing across his face, and Astrid took her chance.

She sprinted right at Mr Finifugal, hoping to lead him away

from Mason. Caught by surprise, she barrelled past, half-running, half-stumbling over the uneven ground.

Mr Finifugal was faster than her. Of course he was – he was a grown man, and she was just a child, and a month ago she'd been living in a shed and had never run full tilt, not like this, never. While he was still several steps behind, she ducked behind a pile of bricks, then dropped to her hands and knees and crawled under an abandoned tarpaulin. Perhaps he would think she was faster than she was, assume she was out of sight already. She lay in the dark, motionless, and tried not to breathe as running footsteps came closer, and then stopped.

Astrid's breath came in short sharp gasps, every muscle taut.

Hopefully Mason and the other boy were close to safety.

She could see Mr Finifugal's shoes in the gap between the tarpaulin and the ground.

Astrid held her breath.

He snatched the tarpaulin off her. Before she could move, he grabbed her hair.

20

Astrid's shriek was so ear-splitting that it even frightened her.

He'd got her. There was no point in screaming, none at all, and yet she couldn't stop – at least, not until he lifted her like a ragdoll, his hand around her throat.

Astrid could feel the flutter of her heartbeat.

'Stop screaming,' Mr Finifugal said, the hiss of his voice low and deadly.

Astrid trembled, and swayed, and stopped. 'Your wife,' she croaked. Anything to distract him. Anything.

It worked. Mr Finifugal's eyes narrowed.

'Did you know that the Overlords don't allow non-Librae adults to live in London Overhead? Too dangerous, even with

221

the nets. And we must keep the Librae world secret, mustn't we?'

His hand tightened around her throat, and her vision flickered.

'Any number of Librae in London Overhead have families living on the ground. It isn't exactly beneficial for the family in question. I couldn't tell my wife where I really was. She couldn't accompany me. She could never understand half my life, or see my wings, or join me in the sky. But love – love is powerful. Love can take hold of you and shake out your logic and your dreams and your beliefs, and leave you instead with a flame at your core. Not just the passion – that comes and goes. The flame of homecoming. A hearth fire where you can warm yourself and cook your dinner and find rest and comfort.'

He paused.

'I love my wife,' he said, with a rasp. 'And my wife is dying. She has days left.'

'You want – you want her to fly,' Astrid whispered.

Mr Finifugal laughed. The laughter shifted into a sob a moment later. 'Fly?' he said. 'I'd settle for walking. For sitting upright. I'd settle for one more sentence from her. No. There was a time when I would have liked my wife to fly, but she never would have accepted wings. Not wings that belonged to someone else.'

'Then *why*?' Astrid wheezed. Every word that she spoke hurt, caustic and agonising, his grip tight around her neck.

'My daughter,' Mr Finifugal said, and his face crumpled.

In a flash, Astrid understood. Elise! That was who she was, and why she'd acted so strangely.

'I hoped for a Librae child; someone who'd be able to move freely between our worlds. And Elise was born just in time. But we've waited, and waited. No wings. And no mother, soon. I would move to London Underfoot for her, of course. I would do anything for her. But she'd never be allowed to live with me. Not after this.' His face spasmed, then produced a bleak and toothy parody of a smile. 'I've spent everything on this experiment. For her. I don't have a penny, a job, a home to give her. I've lost everything working towards this.'

'Being poor doesn't mean you can't be her dad,' Astrid said.

'Perhaps not,' Mr Finifugal said. 'But kidnapping?' He gave a bitter bleat of laughter. 'My days down here are numbered. I'll be in jail within the week. Those children have seen my face. Thanks to you.'

Distantly, Astrid heard a scuffle and a quickly stifled exclamation. Quiet, yet Mr Finifugal heard it too. His head whipped around, and he dropped Astrid and deployed. Vulture wings leapt from his shoulders like a pair of well-used feather dusters, grey and greasy with age.

He swooped upwards. Astrid didn't wait. She couldn't help Mason now. She ran again, and there was a roar, the loudest roar she'd ever heard, and a shriek too, high and unending and inhuman.

It grew louder, louder and louder.

There was a wall of translucent plastic sheeting, swaying a little. She dove through it into a tunnel – and the sound was filling her ears, filling her head.

A train.

It burst through the tunnel like a dragon – a train filled with people, their faces tranquil and placid – didn't they know what was happening? Didn't they know that Mr Finifugal was near, with his desperation and his grief?

If there was a train, there would be train stations, and there would be people, and there would be safety.

She crouched for a second, lost in indecision, panicked. It was dangerous to go on the tracks. But he could be—

Wingbeats. Mr Finifugal was coming. He must have given up on Mason. Mason had got away, and Astrid felt a swift hiccup of triumph, which dispersed a second later as his shadow streaked across the floor, his wingbeats loud, as loud as the train, great concussions of air. He was coming.

And his voice called out, loud and distinct, as though he was standing right next to her.

'You've got wings too, though they're still deep inside. But you won't for long.'

Horror was churning within Astrid, boiling over, paralysing.

He's going to take my wings. He's going to take my wings and he's going to stick them on his daughter, and I will never fly and I will never do anything, ever again, never see Pent again, Mason, Tristopher, anyone, and Mama. I will never see Mama again.

The tunnel was perilous. But it was a way out.

She leapt down onto the tracks.

The train's red lights vanished as it moved around a bend. Astrid stumbled after it, half blind, those two red lights still imprinted on her vision like the eyes of a monster.

She ran down the middle, avoiding the rails – what if they electrocuted her? She slid and slithered and fell once. As she scrambled to her feet, she looked back and saw Mr Finifugal.

His wings filled the tunnel, and his hands were outstretched, and Astrid's scream came bubbling forth again.

She would rather be crushed by a train than die wingless, broken.

And as though in response to her desperate thought, a rumble came from underground.

Mr Finifugal, behind, made a grab for her.

And just as he almost had her, his fingers brushing her back, she tripped, landing chin-first on a rail. She bit her tongue and her mouth filled up with blood, but Mr Finifugal's momentum had carried him past her, and now he was looking for a way to escape as well, because the approaching train was seconds away – seconds away . . .

A green light, winking in the darkness. EXIT. Astrid flung herself at it. The door didn't give way, but it was set within an alcove. She flattened herself into the space, and half a second later, the train thundered past.

It was there and gone very quickly, but the clangour still resounded in her ears, her head jangling like Starminster's bells.

She wrenched at the door until it swung open and let Astrid out into a maintenance passage.

No good. Mr Finifugal would track her in a second, if he'd escaped the train – and there was plenty of space above it. She needed somewhere with people. Anywhere – anyone. Anyone who would save her life.

Her shambling run was pathetic, but it was all that her worn-out muscles could manage. Her lungs were tight, sweat streaming into her eyes, blurring her vision, the light shimmering and distorting.

Behind her, the door from the tunnel opened quietly, but she still sensed it. Mr Finifugal was trying to be stealthy. That scared her just as much as the noise. He was approaching, and once she was in his grip, she didn't have a hope.

She shouldered her way through another door, and barrelled out into a station. Blackfriars, the name emblazoned everywhere. Blackfriars wasn't busy, but it wasn't deserted, either; she could see a couple up ahead on the escalator. The station was open to the cold night air. Astrid lurched, disorientated.

If she reached the couple, she could ask them to call the police. She leapt onto the escalator and began to climb, step after step, her legs leaden and weak.

She slipped into a memory – walking up a staircase in London Overhead, the stars shining out above her, and the city below her, like a flamboyant jewellery box . . .

No. Snap out of it. He's coming.

The couple above stepped off the escalator. A voice rang out over the Tannoy, reminding the passengers to stand behind a yellow line. There must be more people up there on the concourse.

They would help her.

She put on an extra burst of speed, and she was out, out in Blackfriars Station, which looked banal and officious.

Except for one thing. Her face was everywhere. Papering the walls, staring down from the advertising screens, her dark eyes looking seriously out at the passers-by.

Come home, Astrid. Have you seen Astrid? Where is Astrid Crossley? Find Astrid.

Astrid is missing. Astrid is missing. Astrid is missing.

She could also see a handful of posters featuring photographs of the other children, the ones she'd found in the hospital beds. The round face of the boy who'd gone with Mason was grinning sweetly out of his poster. *Chamberlain Come Home.*

Where had the couple gone? She stared around – there had to be someone to help her. Where was the ticket inspector, the station staff?

Apart from the posters, staring down at her, the station was deserted.

Astrid screamed, screamed out as loud as she could. But no one came. No one was at Blackfriars tonight.

The percussion of wingbeats, matching the thud of her heart. Mr Finifugal. In a second, he would swoop out of the escalator's mouth, and he would have her.

He could get her right here, and no one would help her.

Astrid began to run again, and as Mr Finifugal burst into the hall, his wings blocking out the overhead lights, she dived into a narrow walkway.

As she ran, she became aware that the shifting blackness outside the window, with its patches of undulating light, was the Thames. She could smell the river, its salty, primal stink, like the sweat of a dragon, and she had almost crossed it when Mr Finifugal's arms wrapped around her legs.

Astrid fell, a dramatic, flying fall, skidding across the floor and out into the station on the other side, leaving a great painful friction burn across one cheek. He pinned her down, his forearm crushing the back of her neck.

'Please,' Astrid wheezed out. 'Please.'

She wanted to say more – to show him she was a person, a child, like his daughter – but she had neither breath nor strength.

'You haven't fledged yet,' Mr Finifugal said. 'But the wings are there, inside you. That's my hypothesis.'

'You're – hurting me.'

'My Elise – my Elise needs wings, or she won't have a family any more,' Mr Finifugal said, as though he was trying to persuade himself. 'Yours will have to do. You're her last chance.'

'Don't . . . don't,' Astrid gasped.

Mr Finifugal was going to take her wings, her poor wings that had never seen the light of day.

She couldn't take a breath, couldn't fill her lungs, and everything she could see was shrinking down to a pinprick.

Out of nowhere, an enormous flying blur collided with Mr Finifugal. He was thrown off her, landing on the stone floor a couple of metres away. Astrid wanted to get up, but her limbs would not obey her, and she lay paralysed, staring at a pair of dappled owl wings and the man they belonged to.

Mr Strangley.

He stood, motionless, between the Headmaster and Astrid. Astrid couldn't see Mr Strangley's expression, but she could see Mr Finifugal's – a scorching grimace of rage and hatred and grief.

Mr Finifugal got slowly to his feet, his wings opening once again.

'Let the girl be,' Mr Strangley said.

'I need wings,' Mr Finifugal said. 'I need wings for Elise.'

'I know, Ferguson,' Mr Strangley said, and his voice was filled with compassion. 'But this is not the answer.'

'What is, then?' Mr Finifugal shouted. His voice echoed around the station. 'You think I'd let my daughter go to strangers?'

'Astrid,' Mr Strangley said quietly, 'go outside.'

Astrid got up, her feet prickling and her head swimming.

'No!' Mr Finifugal shouted, and he dived at Mr Strangley, a scalpel glittering in his hand.

Mr Strangley grunted. He fell to his knees.

Astrid ran.

She made it outside, the air brisk and fresh against her face.

And two arms closed about her waist.

She was lifted from the ground with a long, lilting scream, hauled over the wall to the Thames, then into a great swooping dive that pulled up just as they seemed about to splash into the river. Astrid's scream kept on coming, staccato as she paused for breath and then started again, screams like air pouring out of her, until she heard the shout from behind her.

'It's all right, Astrid! It's Mr Strangley! You're safe now.'

Then they were scudding along the surface of the river. Astrid caught a glimpse of her own face, pale and rapt, in the water.

They flew beneath a bridge, dark and echoing, then burst out upon the water. Mr Strangley's wings beat, and his arms were strong around her. They were gaining height, soaring above London Underfoot.

Even this late at night, the city was full of life, and Astrid could hear London – languages she didn't know, the rumble of traffic, one high, hysterical laugh.

Then further upwards, through the bridges and platforms of London Overhead until they were above that too, and London Overhead was as small as its city foundation. Astrid's heart swelled with love. Her spiderweb city, delicate, and fragile, and perfect.

She was sobbing as they flew, weeping with delayed shock and relief. And perhaps she was sobbing for the Headmaster too, with his frozen expression of hopelessness, with the name *Elise* like a jewel on his tongue.

Astrid's injuries began to sing out for attention – the friction burn on her face, the bitten tongue, along with a ferocious pain in her ribs that stabbed with every breath she took. Her shoulders ached and burned.

Mr Strangley headed for the Second Flower, the orchid dazzling with light. Carefully, as though she were made of glass, he set her down on the manicured lawn outside. Then he fell forward, a spreading bloodstain on his shirt.

Seconds later, people were streaming from the building, from the skies, and Astrid crumpled to the ground like a marionette with severed strings. She gazed up at the strangers until she found Mrs Wairi's face.

Mrs Wairi leaned over her.

'Astrid,' she said, and her voice sounded faint and faraway. 'It's all right.'

'Did they all come home?' Astrid asked. Her voice echoed, singing back to her: *home, home, home.*

'Yes. The Librae children left the Underfooters at police stations, and returned to London Overhead. Everyone is safe.'

'Mason?'

'Everyone, Astrid.'

'Good,' Astrid said. 'That's good.'

The crowd pulled back to make way for someone. A woman in white – a doctor. She dabbed something that stung on Astrid's cheek, and asked her about pain. Astrid pointed to her ribs, and she began to examine them, pressing down.

Unexpectedly, Astrid heard a grating sound, and agony exploded in her side. As she lay there, flat on her back in the grass, a few faint stars above her, it began to rain.

21

It turned out that Mr Finifugal had fractured a couple of Astrid's ribs. Astrid was sternly informed that this was an injury best healed by resting, or as Pent termed it, loafing around for a bit.

Pent had no objection to some vicarious loafing, though she was most put out when she realised that Astrid would not be dancing at Rain Muster. But she dragged her along anyway, trussed up in Pent's spare waterproofs, the very next night. The first night of Rain Muster was dedicated to Rainsong, and Pent had bagged them a swing earlier that night by leaving a 'WET PAINT' sign on it.

'How very dishonest of you,' Astrid said, sitting down.

'I'll have you know that this is the best seat in the house,' Pent said, adjusting the umbrella to shelter them both.

She was right. Daylight was fading from the sky, but Astrid could still see the sunshine-coloured flowerbeds on the top level of the Hanging Gardens: violas of buttery gold, dahlias a hundred brimstone shades. Rain bucketed down, sending their complex mathematical petals into a wild dance.

The choir was gathering to sing.

'Look at Mason,' Pent said with a giggle. 'All swanky in his robes.'

'I didn't know Mason could sing.'

The choir began to sing. At first together, their voices lifting and falling in harmony. Then Mason sang alone, his voice sweet and yearning, imploring the rain to fall, to fill up the cisterns, to cure the thirst of the Overheaders. Astrid and Pent listened, their swing swaying as the rain continued to pour.

When the choir finished, Astrid and Pent climbed off their swing to get food. Pent carefully rearranged the 'WET PAINT' sign.

'No one's going to fall for that now,' Astrid said, and she was right. Within ten seconds of their departure, a group of Lower Flights students were sitting on the swing.

'Disgraceful,' Pent muttered. 'And with your broken ribs.'

'Don't worry about it,' Astrid said.

They went down the spiral staircase, draped with vines, to

the stalls on the lower level. Pent bought Astrid a glass of fizzy water and a sourdough bread bowl filled with rich, creamy clam chowder, which she claimed was traditional Rain Muster fare. 'Water, obviously, and soup. It's all about the liquid. My dad hates it. He says it's totally insufficient to feed an adult male.'

'What did your parents say when you came home?'

'Oh,' Pent said, her smile faltering, 'they cried. A lot. Mum's been sleeping in my room. I keep waking up and thinking I'm back in . . . there.'

'I'm sorry,' Astrid said. 'I know it's not enough, but I . . . I really am.'

'It's not your fault, Astrid. It's Finifugal's fault. Just like your broken ribs.'

They passed the food tent, puffing out delicious aromas of every variety of soup: French onion, black bean, avgolemono, broccoli and stilton, lobster bisque, matzoh ball. Astrid lingered over the steaming vats and admired the heaping piles of loaves – a dozen varieties at least. Pretzels and bagels were strung up overhead like bunting, hot and fresh, and every so often, the stall keeper would raise his scissors to cut one down for a customer.

'Let's take a look at the remnant stalls,' Pent said.

'Remnant stalls?'

Pent waved a hand at a stall that was all slim shelves, featuring small paintings and pots and sculptures.

'People make miniature art from their leftover art supplies.' She stopped, picking up a tiny golden pineapple no larger than her fingernail. 'Delivered by your good self?'

'I imagine so,' Astrid said.

The stallkeeper waved through the narrow shelves, and they recognised Merchant Abebe, dressed in amethyst oilsilk. 'My couriers,' he said with a smile. 'Go on, keep it, Penelope. Goodness knows, you earned it. And you can choose something too, Astrid.'

They thanked him, and Astrid considered a teapot the size of a thimble, a watercolour London cityscape, and a glass seashell, before she selected a star carved from mother-of-pearl, a spiny little thing that felt oddly warm and alive in the palm of her hand.

They found a sheltered bench to finish their food, their remnant art safely secreted in their pockets.

The clam chowder was perfect – warm and filling and salty as the ocean. When they'd finished the soup, Astrid and Pent tore their sourdough bowls apart and devoured them.

Mason landed nearby, shaking his wings out like umbrellas, and bought a tureen of cock-a-leekie soup.

They waved, and he came over, wings still showily wide. 'All right, ladies? Did you enjoy my dulcet tones, beckoning in the rain and so forth?'

'You're not supposed to be flying in the open!' Pent blurted. 'You're supposed to have completed forty hours with Mrs Warburton before you're safe to fly alone.'

'What can I say?' Mason said. 'I wasn't fond of formal education even before the Headmaster kidnapped me to steal my wings, and you'd better believe I don't like it any better now. Besides, I'm fine. Took a while to get my flying instincts going, but I have it completely under control now.'

A gust of wind caught his wings and knocked him over sideways. He climbed up, folding his wings away and laughing as if he'd done it on purpose, without a jot of embarrassment.

'How are you, Astrid?' His gaze was sharp and compassionate.

'All right,' Astrid said, glancing away. 'Glad you made it out of Smithfield.'

'I should have come back for you,' Mason said. 'I'm sorry I didn't. I abandoned you.' He laughed. Then his face straightened out, and he said quietly, 'I'm so ashamed of leaving you to face him alone.'

'No,' Astrid said, 'don't be ridiculous. You had to get out, and you had to get Chamberlain out. It was the right thing to do.'

'I'll make it up to you.'

'You can teach me to fly, when I finally fledge,' Astrid suggested, and Mason laughed again.

'I'm not exactly qualified to teach anyone. But you're going to love it. It's better than I ever imagined.'

'Can't wait,' Astrid said, and Pent nodded fervently.

'Let's go see the art exhibition,' Mason said. 'I heard Dr Postlethwaite made something comedically bad.'

They made their way back up the stairs. The top tier had transformed in the hour they'd been gone; lanterns glowed gently among the flowers and in the trees.

'We're meant to take the path,' Pent said, her voice hushed.

The flagstone path meandered and twisted around the garden, and the three of them followed it. The first artwork was a freestanding glass door with water sheeting down it, rippling like satin. Astrid couldn't stop herself from pressing her fingertips to the surface and watching the disrupted flow of water. Faintly, in the glass, she could see her reflection, and dim lights that moved behind the surface.

The next piece was a cairn made of stones, like a fairy pond, surrounded by gnarled bonsai trees. Astrid stopped to look at the teensy metal bench beneath the tree, and the miniature rope swing that dangled from a branch, then noticed a dozen other diminutive details: a mossy rockery growing starry white flowers, a stream with water lilies, small toadstools.

A few exhibits later, they passed through a mushroom garden lit with a string of black light bulbs, every species of mushroom glowing a different colour. Astrid's white T-shirt lit up, intensely purple.

'These exhibits – they're all so beautiful,' Astrid said, looking up at Pent and Mason.

'I can't help noticing that they're rather stretching the idea of "using water in an innovative way", though,' Mason remarked. 'Obviously the mushrooms appreciate the damp, but it isn't exactly the glass train from last year. Now that was innovation.'

As they walked on, they passed paintings that were changing colour as the rain touched them, and a posse of mechanical crimson beetles swimming around a watery obstacle course.

Dr Postlethwaite had made an awkwardly shaped silver clay bowl, and was standing next to it defensively when they walked past.

'It was my first effort at using a pottery wheel,' he snapped before they said a word. 'It's supposed to evoke the raw creativity of the amateur.'

'It's very nice,' Mason said. 'You know in the olden days,

medieval times, when you were young . . . did you ever use playdough at all?'

'Shut your insolent mouth, North,' Dr Postlethwaite said. 'The rudeness of this generation!'

'No, I like it,' Mason said with faux sincerity. 'Can I borrow it for a minute? I want to save some leftover soup for everyone I know.'

Dr Postlethwaite made a furious sweeping gesture, and Pent and Astrid grabbed Mason and marched him away.

'You know, he actually might win,' Pent said. 'There's a prize for collecting the most rainwater, isn't there?'

'Sort of like a participation award,' Astrid said.

'I love Dr Postlethwaite,' Mason said, sighing happily. 'He always takes the Postlebait. Mrs Warburton would have just given me detention and that would have been it, fun over. I would probably attend Starminster more often if it was just me and Doc Poss. Slanging matches have always been my favourite kind of lessons.'

They moved around another bend and were confronted by a towering statue. It was made of stained glass and lit from within.

A mother and a daughter, arms around each other, locked in an eternal embrace. Their stained-glass eyes were shut.

Next to it, the plaque read: *Ferguson Finifugal. For Elise.*

They stood at the feet of the statue in silence. Astrid couldn't take her eyes from the daughter's face. Even though she was made from glass, everything in her posture and expression was real. Rainwater streamed down her glass cheeks. Astrid felt grief break over her, and a wave of pity.

Pent put her arm around Astrid.

'How was your meeting with Mrs Wairi earlier?' she asked.

'Okay,' Astrid said. 'She wanted me to tell her everything that happened.'

'And did you?'

Astrid nodded. She had sat in an office on the Second Flower with a box of tissues and a glass of water in front of her, looking out over the city, and told Mrs Wairi everything. About Smithfield Market, about waking up the students, about the terrifying chase through the railway tunnel and station, about Mr Finifugal's dying wife and his desperation to be with his daughter.

'Did you mention there must have been a mystery accomplice on the ground – whoever Finifugal was messaging?'

'She thinks it was Elise or . . . or her mum. But I'm still not sure. If Finifugal was writing to Elise . . . I think he'd have written something a little bit more . . . loving.'

There was a pause, though music was still audible from below.

'Did you tell her you felt sorry for him?'

Astrid stared out across the Hanging Gardens.

'I . . . sort of. I felt sorry for Elise, mostly. And her mum. Mrs Wairi said they haven't found him yet. He's disappeared into London Underfoot. A committee of Overlords went to his wife's address, but he's gone, and so has Elise.'

'What about his wife?'

'She died,' Astrid said. 'Her name was Odette. I think he stayed with her until she passed away, then left with Elise before he could be arrested.'

'It's awful,' Pent said. 'But what he was planning was awful, too.'

'I know.' The rain fell in silvery slashes, catching the light of the twinkling lanterns. 'I know it was. I heard Fred and Bethany are having nightmares. I just wish someone could have helped him before he started – before he couldn't see another way out.'

'He made his own choices,' Mason said quietly.

Mama had made her choices too, difficult ones that were hard to understand. She'd chosen that lonely childhood for Astrid. But Astrid believed that Mama had made her choices out of love. Even if it didn't make sense, and even if it didn't make up for the years she'd missed, she knew Mama had never wanted to hurt her.

Astrid took off her hood, and lifted her face to the sky. The rain poured down, heavy soaking rain that dripped like sap from the ends of her hair. And no one needed to know whether the wetness on her face was rainwater, or something else.

'Anyway,' Pent said bracingly, 'we're back in lessons once Rain Muster ends. I have *so* many questions to ask Barker. I'm planning to start with why the Overlords exist and also why they're totally incompetent.'

'I may actually attend that lesson,' Mason remarked.

'I suppose they felt sorry for Finifugal,' Astrid said. 'They knew about his wife, so they decided not to challenge him on how he ran Starminster.'

'That was a mistake,' Mason said. 'If they'd pulled him up earlier, maybe this wouldn't have happened.' He shook his head. 'I don't understand it. His beloved wife and daughter weren't Librae, and yet he seemed to look down on us for not having fledged yet.'

'I think he felt like we were wasting the chance they never got,' Astrid said quietly.

'Either way,' Mason said, 'one thing's for sure. No one's sitting on the floor any more. Everyone's equal, wings or no wings.'

'Strangley was right,' Pent said, 'even though he caused us a lot of trouble. We belong here. We're all going to fly one of these days.'

'Is Strangley okay, by the way?' Mason asked.

'Mrs Wairi says he's out of danger.' Astrid swallowed down a new sob, thinking about him. He had saved her life.

Unexpectedly, it began to hail, great chunks of ice hurtling down. Mason deployed, raising a protective wing over the heads of Pent and Astrid.

A crash. One of the hailstones had hit the sculpture, smashing into the mother's shoulder, shattering it.

'The statue,' Astrid said, moving forward, her hands outstretched. 'It's going to be ruined!'

Mason pulled her back into the shelter of his wings. 'Let it be, Astrid,' he said, and his voice was gentle. 'You've done everything you can. You saved the wings of six people.' He paused. 'I can never repay you. But it's time to forget about Finifugal and his daughter.'

They retreated to the lower level of the Hanging Gardens and ate spectrum chocolate mousse out of cocktail glasses, with swirls of darkest chocolate and cream.

Later, they overheard a woman mention to another that a few of the art exhibits had been destroyed.

'Glass,' said the woman, with a shrug. 'Always risky.'

22

The next day, Astrid woke with a clear and fully formed plan in her mind. She set off for the Second Flower, carrying a folder.

The Second Flower was ultra-modern and sleek, a coral reef of scurrying life. Formal meetings were taking place in alcoves, and crystalline offices protruded from the walls and ceiling as well as the floor, supported by poison-green malachite pillars.

A woman sat serenely in the centre of the atrium within a circular glass dome, like a soap bubble.

Astrid tapped on the glass and said, 'Can I see Councillor Paulson?'

The woman escorted her to a glass office towards the back

of the flower. Councillor Paulson sat behind a vast granite desk that made him look rather shrunken, writing something down.

Astrid knocked, and Councillor Paulson said, 'Enter!' without looking up.

She walked up to the desk, opened her folder, and placed it in front of him.

'How may I help you?' Councillor Paulson said. 'I'm afraid I know very little about this Finifugal business; you'd be better served by speaking to Mrs Wairi, if you can find the dear woman.'

'It's not about that,' Astrid said. 'You're in charge of London Overhead's infrastructure, I understand.'

A hint of annoyance played around Councillor Paulson's mouth. 'Correct.'

'This is a list of the hazards around the Fourth Flower,' Astrid said. She pushed the folder towards him. 'There are more than fifty there, and that's just for a small area.'

Paulson flipped the cover shut. 'Right, well, thanks muchly and all that. I'll take a look when I get a moment.'

Astrid opened the folder again. 'Unfledged students walk along these routes every day,' she said. 'And you'll notice that I've highlighted these areas. Looks like wear and tear on the nets.'

'Good gracious, girl, I'm horribly busy.'

'I appreciate that,' Astrid said. 'This is why I'm offering to deal with some of these hazards. The ones that are underlined have already been fixed, and the ones marked with asterisks are manageable for me. A handful, like the net problem, will require professional maintenance.'

Councillor Paulson relaxed into his chair. 'How . . . helpful.'

'I'm afraid I will be charging you a fee.'

'A fee?'

'I need an income,' Astrid said steadily. 'So that I can buy school supplies and clothing. I don't want much, and in return, I will monitor the main pedestrian routes around the city. I'll fix what I can, and I'll document larger issues so that you arrange for those to be seen to.'

Councillor Paulson sputtered for a bit, but Astrid flicked to the back of her folder and showed him the fee she intended to charge. 'As you can see, this monthly stipend will cover my time and the supplies I need.'

'I still view this as unnecessary,' he bleated.

'If you don't deal with these issues,' Astrid said, 'an unfledged child will fall to their death, and you will be held responsible.'

A long silence unfolded. Astrid looked out of the window. She could see a bridge where she'd made some repairs, smoothing down the sharp edges of peeling paint with sandpaper so that you could grip the banister safely.

'I think,' she said, 'that this arrangement could be beneficial to us both.'

'Fine,' Councillor Paulson said crossly. 'I accept your proposition.'

Astrid smiled at him.

'Is that all? Some of us have rather a lot of work to do.'

'There's one more thing,' Astrid said. 'I want to live in Starminster.'

'For heaven's sake, girl!'

'There's space for me,' Astrid said, settling into the chair. 'If not, I'd be tempted to charge for the repairs I've already completed. Which are numerous.'

'What's wrong with the Fourth Flower?'

'Nothing. But I belong at Starminster.'

Councillor Paulson stared at her, his knuckles white as he gripped his Mont Blanc fountain pen. 'Very well,' he snapped. 'I need a whisky. Meet me at Starminster in two hours.'

He stormed out of the office. Astrid went into the bustling atrium. She squared her shoulders and pushed through the crowd.

A voice called her name. It was Mrs Wairi, her expression inscrutable.

'I've been looking for you everywhere, Astrid. There's someone here to see you.'

Astrid glanced at the massive clock that hung from the ceiling. She had plenty of time to get to Starminster.

She followed Mrs Wairi into her office, then stopped dead.

Mama.

*   *   *

She stood by the window, looking out on London Overhead. As Astrid entered, she turned.

Her face looked different in daylight. There were shadows across her features that made her look harsher, older, and her hair was more silver than gold.

'Astrid,' she said, her voice familiar as candlelight. The comfort of Mama, responsibility sliding from her shoulders. Dreadful tenderness in Astrid's heart.

Astrid spoke. 'Are you sending me back, Mrs Wairi?'

'No,' Mrs Wairi said. 'I'm going to give you a moment with your mother. I'll be outside.' She left, closing the door gently behind her.

Mama lifted her arms, then let them drop when Astrid didn't move.

Astrid became aware of an unexpected feeling, buried deep – sorrow, and a simmer of fury.

'You knew I was Librae,' Astrid said. 'So you locked me up.'

Mama's face went very still.

'My whole life. My whole childhood.'

'For you,' Mama said at last, haltingly, carefully. 'I – I wanted to save you. From London Overhead. From being Librae.'

'Why?'

'There's a lot you don't know, Astrid.'

Astrid looked away.

Words slipped through her mind, unsaid. *I don't know why I had to live without sunlight for years, years that slid away like pearls on a string, never to be retrieved. I don't understand why I could never walk down a street on a summer's day with my hand in yours. I don't know why you stole a decade of my life. I will never be small, and free, and earthbound, and ignorant. It is lost to me.*

'Explain it to me, then. I . . . I can't understand why you locked me up.'

Mama gave a shaky little smile.

'Very well. Twelve years ago, after months of pleading and paperwork, I came to London Overhead to visit my father. My visit was a rare exception to the laws. It would never have been allowed now, and I believe it was only permitted then because of Dad's connections with the Ceramicists. My father was a Librae, you see. I was not. But I loved being here at once.' Her eyes turned dreamy, and Mama pressed her palms against the window, London Overhead ethereal in the rainy mist. 'London Overhead. Like a layer of shining oil, floating atop the dirty puddle of London. I haven't returned until today.'

'Why?' Astrid said.

'There was . . . an incident, some years ago. Immigration laws became much, much stricter.' Mama hesitated, then said quickly, words spilling out fast, 'I met your father during that visit, Astrid. I returned home, and soon after, I discovered I was pregnant. My mother died before you were born. After her funeral, Dad flew away, and I never saw him again.'

Astrid's head swam. Relatives. Grandfather, grandmother.

And a father. A Librae father.

A family, beyond her and Mama.

'I was young. Young and grieving. You were born prematurely, just within Librae season. And I made an awful mistake, a product of fear, and stupidity, and weakness. I looked at your tiny body, and I had to protect you. So I locked you up with the rhubarb. I was terrified of losing you, Astrid. Terrified you would grow wings and fly away the moment I took my eyes from you.'

'You could have kept me with you,' Astrid said quietly. She could almost smell the sweet air of the childhood she'd never had. Golden fields, and the rough fleece of sheep. Her hand in Mama's, with the sky stretching wide and empty above them.

Mama shook her head, and the phantom childhood vanished. 'I'd learned from my father that there are mysteries of Libraekind that we don't understand. If a Librae child never sees starlight, their wings . . . their wings will never grow.' Her voice shook so much that Astrid could hardly understand her. 'I hid you away in darkness, so you would never have to choose between me and the sky.'

Astrid was on her feet before she knew it, fists clenched. 'So just because you couldn't have wings, you decided to steal them from me?'

Mama stood as well, her hands reaching out to Astrid like a plant stretching towards the light. 'No, Astrid. It wasn't that simple. Or that cruel. I wasn't in London Overhead for long, but there were mutterings . . . I heard things from my father, and I eavesdropped, and I didn't understand everything, but I knew London Overhead wasn't safe.' She paused. 'Ferguson Finifugal was not yet Headmaster, but even then, he was plotting. Plots that Mrs Wairi tells me are no longer, because of you.

'Finifugal is gone. You'll be safe here now,' Mama said gently. 'And soon your wings should grow. I didn't come to take you back, Astrid. I'm here to apologise. I'm not asking anything of you, my daughter. Not forgiveness, not promises, not love. I just want you to know how sorry I am.'

Another pain, deeper than the ache of her broken ribs.

'Goodbye, darling,' Mama said. Her arms half lifted again, then fell back to her sides. 'Stay safe.' She reached for the doorknob, rubbing her forearm across her eyes.

'Wait,' Astrid said.

Mama turned back, tears glittering on her cheeks.

'You're doing it again,' Astrid said. 'You're making my choices for me. I think it's my turn to make a decision. Don't you?'

Mama nodded.

Astrid swallowed. She wanted her next words to ring out firm and steady, but her voice broke halfway through.

'You made a mistake. I forgive you for it. I promise to come home every year, so we can be together. And nothing – nothing can ever stop me loving you.'

She didn't remember how she got there, or who opened their arms first, but Astrid was enveloped in Mama's arms, and her head was pressed against the warm curve of Mama's neck. Both were crying, and with the tears, Astrid felt a kernel within her, a rock-hard kernel of bitterness, dissolve and disappear.

*   *   *

Mrs Wairi came back inside after most of the tears had been shed, and they agreed that Astrid would go home at Christmas.

'We'll have a Christmas tree with real candles,' Mama said. 'Hot chocolate. No rhubarb of any description.'

Astrid walked with Mama and Mrs Wairi back to the Shard. The building stabbed through both cities, like a needle stitching them together, and she remembered that first walk, clutching the railings. Now she knew these steps, and they passed several of her own repairs.

They said goodbye. Astrid felt a prickle of homesickness as she waved to Mama. The sorrow lasted several bridges from the Shard, until she reached a square thick with apple trees and Pent appeared, chomping on an apple.

'How did it go with Paulson?'

'Really well,' Astrid said. 'He's agreed to pay me.'

'I bet he's ripping you off,' Pent said as they began to walk.

'I don't need much,' Astrid said. 'If I make him pay fairly,

I'll have him hassling me continually. But if he thinks he's got one over on me, then I can play it the way I want.'

'Will you slack off, then?'

'No. I'm actually serious about it.' She paused and gave one of the banisters on the wooden bridge an experimental push. 'See? It's rotten. Needs replacing. I want this place to be safer for unfledged children.'

'That's actually noble,' Pent said. 'I'm touched. Also, I got you an apple. Want it?'

'Thanks,' Astrid said. They walked to Starminster together, crunching on their apples, in companionable silence.

'I saw my mum,' Astrid said.

'Right,' Pent said. 'Happy, sad?'

'Both. But good. Honest.'

'If you want to talk about it, I'm here to listen,' Pent said. 'But if you're not ready yet, that's okay, too.'

'Thanks,' Astrid said.

It was tempting to leave it at that, but friendship, she was discovering, sometimes meant that you had to be brave.

'My mum . . . she kept me locked up. In a rhubarb shed. She was scared I'd fly away. She was trying to protect me. So I had a sort of weird childhood. But I'm going to go home at Christmas, and I – I forgive her.'

Pent reached out and took her hand, squeezing it.

Astrid felt tears gather again as she squeezed back. Pent was her first friend. But to Astrid's enormous surprise, she wasn't her only friend by any means. The new fledglings and the unfledged children hadn't a scrap of resentment about their imprisonment. If anything, they'd gained respect for Astrid.

Her life was full of anticipation now, where once it had held only the drudgery of routine. Another evening of Rain Muster tonight. Lessons at Starminster next week. New friendships growing every day. Wings, someday.

They reached Starminster, where Councillor Paulson was waiting impatiently on the Stone Gallery.

He said gruffly, 'There's an attic room. The custodial staff of St Paul's have lost the key and more or less forgotten its existence. The only remaining keys belong to us.'

They entered a warren of corridors, so narrow that they had to walk in single file until they reached a door. Councillor Paulson produced a weighty keychain and located a key. After a great deal of dramatic huffing and puffing, he wrenched the door open.

The forgotten room was piled ceiling-high with miscellany. Astrid walked through the room, touching embroidered fabric, and wooden boards inscribed with golden script.

'The door into the main cathedral must remain locked at all times,' Councillor Paulson said. 'But there's an exit hatch, I believe, through the rafters. It leads outside onto the Stone Gallery.'

The room was filled with pigeon rustlings and coos. Every surface was velvet with dust.

'Surely you'd prefer to be with the other children,' Councillor Paulson said.

Astrid looked around. Tendrils of light filtered in from the small leaded window, but the room itself was dark, and crowded, and small.

'No,' she said. 'This is perfect.'

'Good show,' Councillor Paulson muttered. He departed in a cloud of ill-suppressed indignation.

* * *

For the rest of the day, Astrid and Pent worked hard. They dusted and scrubbed and chucked sweepings of dust into the London breeze. They laid a tapestry on the floor as a carpet. They set up an ornate woodwormed altar as a desk and dressing table.

Already, the attic felt more friendly. They cleaned the tiny window and flung it open, letting in fresh air. Pent had found a box of candles, and she put one inside a thurible.

Finally, they took all the fabric they could find, altar cloths, velvet curtains and the embroidered surplices of bishops, and carried them outside onto the Stone Gallery to beat the dust out of them. Pent didn't allow Astrid to help. 'Your ribs are rubbish now, remember?'

Pent pushed two heavy antique pews together and piled on thick layers of fabric. She took off her shoes and climbed into it to test for comfort.

'Not bad,' she said. 'Yes, I think I could sleep comfortably on this weird bed.'

Astrid lay down next to her. The candle in the thurible threw filigree shadows onto the ceiling and gave off a faint reek of incense.

'A liminal space,' Pent said.

'What?'

'It's a place on the threshold. Neither London Overhead nor London Underfoot. Neither above nor below. Neither sky nor earth.'

'I like it. We should call it that,' Astrid said. 'The Liminal Attic.'

Already, she could tell that she would sleep well here; that the candlelight and the solid roof overhead would help her to rest. Her own room. And she could leave it anytime she wanted.

That was what they did next. Astrid and Pent clambered across rafters, and through the hatch onto the Stone Gallery. It was raining more heavily, and the wind had picked up. Astrid climbed to the top of the mossy old staircase that led up into London Overhead. The flowers stood tall; the city dazzled.

Mason was swooping towards them, and Pent was laughing at something Astrid had said.

Astrid opened her arms and closed her eyes to feel the wind against her face. A great gust of wind caught at her hair and sent it streaming out, her hands filling up with rainwater like an offering.

An unexpected prickle of pain. She grimaced, biting down on her lower lip.

Pent touched her arm. 'Astrid, are you okay? Is it your ribs?'

'No, it's . . .'

The burn in her shoulders was worsening by the second. Just like the pain she'd felt when she flew with Mr Strangley. Astrid reached back to touch the skin beneath her shirt, and felt spiny barbs. Feathers, forcing their way through.

It was happening.

Triumph, brief and magical and longed-for. At last.

Astrid laughed, and the sound of her laughter was unrestrained and joyous, pealing out.

'What is it?'

She stood tall and strong, the rain falling down like a blessing, at the edge of her enchanted, suspended city. London's lights glimmered like stars below, and the infinity of stars shone above the clouds, unseen.

'Astrid?' Mason said.

The smile on her face was incandescent. 'I'm fledging,' she said.

Acknowledgements